The trial begins:

Jack Frazier held out his arms as if gathering all the jurors into a bouquet. I felt a little swept up too. "Go back," he said, "go back to a night four and a half years ago. Loretta Gray," he gestured to my mother, "was pregnant. A beautiful low-risk pregnancy with no problems at all. Loretta Gray found herself going into labor, two and a half weeks before her due date." His voice grew much louder and his accent heavier. He filled the entire room, even its cracks, like insulating foam. I felt as if my blood were moving faster through my veins, and my cheeks were warm. The redheaded juror—first row, center seat—stiffened. I hardly blamed her. That kind of intensity could be frightening. And Jack Frazier was right on top of her!

"Loretta Gray's husband was away. Her first child, Ellen, twelve at the time, and who you see before you today at sixteen . . ." For a moment all eyes were on me.

"[The trial] is the heartbeat of the story. . . . Metzger once again demonstrates exceptional skill in building and then peeling back the intricate layers of her characters." —*School Library Journal*

Y0-BBY-644

OTHER PUFFIN BOOKS YOU MAY ENJOY

Beyond Safe Boundaries   Margaret Sacks

Blue Tights   Rita Williams-Garcia

Breaking the Fall   Michael Cadnum

Calling Home   Michael Cadnum

Celebrating the Hero   Lyll Becerra de Jenkins

Dive   Stacey Donovan

The Ear, the Eye and the Arm   Nancy Farmer

Father Figure   Richard Peck

A Hand Full of Stars   Rafik Schami

The Honorable Prison   Lyll Becerra de Jenkins

*How Far Would You Have Gotten If I Hadn't
Called You Back?*   Valerie Hobbs

An Island Like You   Judith Ortiz Cofer

Kiss the Dust   Elizabeth Laird

Let the Circle Be Unbroken   Mildred D. Taylor

No Tigers in Africa   Norman Silver

Over the Water   Maude Casey

The Road to Memphis   Mildred D. Taylor

Roll of Thunder, Hear My Cry   Mildred D. Taylor

Song of Be   Lesley Beake

Teacup Full of Roses   Sharon Bell Mathis

Transport 7-41-R   T. Degens

Traveling On into the Light   Martha Brooks

The Wild Children   Felice Holman

Won't Know Till I Get There   Walter Dean Myers

ellen's case

by Lois Metzger

PUFFIN BOOKS

PUFFIN BOOKS

Published by the Penguin Group

Penguin Books USA Inc., 375 Hudson Street, New York, New York 10014, U.S.A.

Penguin Books Ltd, 27 Wrights Lane, London W8 5TZ, England

Penguin Books Australia Ltd, Ringwood, Victoria, Australia

Penguin Books Canada Ltd, 10 Alcorn Avenue, Toronto, Ontario, Canada M4V 3B2

Penguin Books (N.Z.) Ltd, 182-190 Wairau Road, Auckland 10, New Zealand

Penguin Books Ltd, Registered Offices: Harmondsworth, Middlesex, England

First published in the United States of America by Atheneum Books for Young
Readers, an imprint of Simon & Schuster Children's Publishing Division, 1995
"A Jean Karl Book"
Published in Puffin Books, 1997

1 3 5 7 9 10 8 6 4 2

LIBRARY OF CONGRESS CATALOGING-IN-PUBLICATION DATA

Metzger, Lois.

Ellen's Case / Lois Metzger.

p. cm.

Sequel to: Barry's sister.

Summary: When sixteen-year-old Ellen Gray finds herself attracted to the lawyer
in charge of the malpractice case related to her four-year-old brother's cerebral
palsy, she becomes involved in the trial and gains a new perspective
on her own life and options for her future.

ISBN 0-14-038372-7 (pbk.)

[1. Trials (Malpractice)—Fiction. 2. Cerebral palsy—Fiction.
3. Physically handicapped—Fiction. 4. Brothers and sisters—Fiction.] I. Title.
PZ7.M5677El 1997 [Fic]—dc21 96-53947 CIP AC

Printed in the United States of America

Many thanks to Jean Karl, and to Judy Livingston and Tom Moore. The following people and organizations also gave generously of their time and expertise: The American College of Obstetricians and Gynecologists; Robin Angel of United Cerebral Palsy of New York City, Inc.; Leon Charash, M.D.; Susan Cohen; Joanna Cole; Eleanor Ebel; the Emerson family; Nancy Franklin; the Hon. Ira Gammerman; Tony Hiss; Ann Hobson; Beth J. Lief; Maureen Lynch; Susan Nierenberg, C.N.M.; Lisa Pappanikou of the Sibling Information Network; Gail Paris; the Pollack family; Margaux Poueymirou; Thomas J. Principe, Esq.; Liz Rosenberg; Amy Tonsits; Susan Wald, formerly of The Shield Institute; the Wawrzonek family; the Weitz family; the Young Adult Institute; Judith Zimmer.

To Tony
and to the memory of Mutti,
my grandmother

barry's case

one

"I've taken care of everything," I told Maribeth firmly. This was the last Saturday in June, last summer, and we were about to throw open the doors of Cave, the art gallery Maribeth Ramsey owned in Tribeca, which is downtown in New York City. Outside, it was blisteringly hot, but inside it was cool, hushed, empty, dim—you'd never guess that in half an hour people from all over the city would be crowding in for our new show. "Here's the adjusted price list, all typed up." I flapped several pieces of paper in front of her. "I've reset the lights—aren't they perfect? And I made sure every painting has the exact right title."

Loretta—that's my mother—had told me that at Thursday's opening-night party several titles had been jumbled up. This was such an insult to an artist, I always thought, like putting the wrong name on a tombstone! It never would have happened if I'd been here, but on Thursday I had a fever—one hundred and three. Loretta claimed I'd contracted a kind of homesickness-in-reverse, that I missed my father. An executive officer on a nuclear submarine, he was away on patrol after being home for almost two years. But if Loretta's theory was true, why did I get a fever on my sixteenth birthday back in February, with my father right there beside me?

"Ellen, you're a wonder!" Maribeth—my mother's best friend, and my friend, too—gave me a bear hug. She had on a dress where orange, brown, and red melted together, like an erupting volcano; it had accordion pleats and sleeves that looked like hanging Japanese lanterns.

"Maribeth," I had to ask, "after you wash that dress, don't you have to iron it very carefully? Doesn't it take forever?"

"Oh, honey, it's brand-new—I have no idea. Probably I'll have to dry-clean it for a fortune." That was Maribeth—act now, deal with it later. "Why, want to borrow it sometime?"

"Me? No way! I mean, no, thank you." Since turning sixteen, I'd made a decision, kind of a New Year's resolution on my birthday. Now my hair was all one length, no more bangs or layers or blond streaks—solid brown hair that fell just above my shoulders. I never wore more than two solid colors in a whole outfit. Eight unbroken hours of sleep. Three well-balanced meals a day and no snacks in between. Life was complicated enough. It was time to make my life altogether simple.

"Ellen has not taken care of everything, and Ellen is not a wonder." This came from Sam, Maribeth's eighteen-year-old son. He'd been in the gallery's other room, but with all the quiet emptiness in between, he'd heard us—or he'd been eavesdropping. "Look how she's drowned that painting with light."

My neck stiffened as if I'd been sitting all afternoon in the front row at the movies. Sam was pointing at the painting I loved best in the show, a nighttime forest scene called "Lost in the Familiar." I could almost feel the wet earth beneath my feet, smell the damp leaves, see the curved branches rustling like the fans of slave girls. Several times before, we'd exhibited this artist, a Brazilian woman, and always her work had been bright and lively, startlingly blue lakes pierced with light—white light that when you started closely at it contained bits of green and brown. But this show was all darkness and gloom. What had happened to her? *Something*, clearly. Something painful. But these paintings were her best.

"Too little light," I informed Sam, "and that painting will melt into the wall." Cave was kept deliberately dark, except for spotlights on the paintings. "I bet it was your fault Thursday night when the titles were wrong!"

"Don't bet," Sam said. "Besides, with these titles, no one even noticed."

"Sam is right." Maribeth sighed. "No one noticed. And the titles were my fault."

But I thought "Lost in the Familiar" was an enigmatically beautiful title, and didn't suit any other painting.

Sam adjusted the spotlight with his right hand. He's tall, and his curly hair is completely gray, and his left hand is forever clenched in a fist. That, and a slightly awkward leaning to the left, noticeable mostly when he walks, are the only signs that he has cerebral palsy. When my brother, Barry, walks, he looks drunk. Barry also has what's called mild CP, though his case is more severe than

Sam's. Now that he's four, Barry has trouble with the toothpaste tube, and usually a huge glob explodes out. He can feed himself crackers, but they crumble in his hands. He needs help dressing and eating; he wears knee pads because he's always falling; he still wears diapers; and if you tell him, "Barry, close the bedroom door and bring me your slippers," he will forget one or the other.

Never mind about Barry—the way Sam acted, Sam was the only handicapped person in the universe, and how he suffered!

"Better?" Sam challenged me, but his tone was surprisingly friendly.

"Different," I said, giving it a sideways glance.

"Better," Sam insisted. "Why won't you agree with me when I'm right? But no—whenever I say black, Ellen Gray says white."

"I do not!" I said.

Sam grinned. "See?"

Maribeth let out a loud laugh. "You two sound married," she said.

Sam's grin disappeared, and he stalked out of the gallery. As far as I knew, Sam had never had a girlfriend.

I was about to reset the light when I had to stop. I could see deeper into the forest—there was a sliver of a moon just beyond one branch. "It is better," I told Maribeth in a low voice. "Sam knows his stuff, doesn't he?"

"He's been around paintings his whole life," Maribeth said. "You're learning." Maribeth had tied her frizzy red hair back into a scarf, but it kept on escaping like water spraying from an open hydrant. She had round, bright, dark eyes, at the same time sharp and gentle. "Don't be so hard on yourself, Ellen."

Was wanting to be good at something a fault? If so, I longed to be the world's most flawed human being.

"Loretta told me you practically ran the eleventh grade this year, all by yourself."

"Don't I wish!" I said. But I had only a few extra-curricular activities. I was captain of the softball team, and had created the school's recycling program ("Don't Waste Waste"), and after school worked at Loretta's library and here at the gallery. "I don't do all that much," I said. "I still have time to visit my grandparents every other weekend."

Maribeth shook her head. "It's too much, Ellen. Maybe I should fire you—then you'd have your Saturdays free. But you're too good—you take care of everything."

It was exactly the right thing to say to me. More than anything, that's what I wanted to be when I grew up—a person who could take care of everything. It didn't matter what I would actually do for a living. Still, I couldn't help saying, "Sam doesn't think so." Why did I let him get to me, anyway?

"Sam's a little hard on you," Maribeth said, "because he's so hard on himself."

This made absolutely no sense. What did I have to do with Sam's relationship to Sam?

All afternoon I sat on a high stool behind an oak desk with my list of prices, and never got bored staring at people staring at paintings. Some only pretended to look. Some went into a hypnotic trance. Some were so aware of themselves that really every painting could have been a mirror.

A few paintings sold, but no one even asked about "Lost in the Familiar." I could almost see it in my room, reflected in the mirror over my bureau. There sure was room for it—all my posters had come down in February. I had two hundred and twenty-seven dollars saved up—was that enough for a down payment on a seven thousand dollar painting? But the painting would never appear on my wall. All my money was for Barry's future.

Toward the end of the afternoon, a middle-aged man in too small jeans and with too much chest showing came up to me and asked, "Are you a cave dweller?"

I blinked at him. "What?"

"You're here," he said with a toothy smile, his dimples so deep it looked as though a knife had cut them out. "This place is called Cave. Are you a cave dweller?"

I kept my face so straight, you'd think I smiled about as often as we had an eclipse. "Are you interested in purchasing a painting?"

"You're awfully pretty," he said. "But you don't know it, do you?"

I could list the people who did. Maribeth said I looked like a Spanish princess; Loretta thought I was a double of Barbara Stanwyck, an old-time movie actress; Ray, my boyfriend, said I was "as lovely as the pause in the air before someone got a joke and laughed"; my best friend, Roz, said I was as pretty as I wanted to be (whatever that meant); and then there was Sam, who said, rather off the subject, maybe, that if you crossed a mule and a cactus, you'd get me. I didn't much care. Since February, basically, when I looked at the mirror, it was to make sure I didn't have spinach stuck in my teeth. I said, "If you're not interested in purchasing a painting—"

"I'm interested in purchasing you a drink."

I was going to make those dimples disappear, fast. "I'm sixteen years old," I told him. I could have said I had a boyfriend, but it never even occurred to me.

"Oh—well—sorry," he stammered. "You look much older. Must be a trick of the light." And he spun around. There was a large comb in his back pocket—the jeans were so tight I could see every tooth. I'll probably remember him always, I thought, for being so utterly forgettable.

Just before closing, Sam showed up again. "Isn't it ironic," he said to me, "how artists supposedly live simple, unconventional, to-thine-own-self-be-true kinds of lives, yet they depend on rich bastards to buy their work."

"Ironic," I agreed. "See? Sometimes you say black and I say black."

Sam bowed deeply. "I stand corrected. I stand to the left, but I stand."

I laughed casually, but really I was shocked to the core. Had Sam ever joked about himself? Especially about his cerebral palsy? Knowing Sam reminded me of something I'd once read about training tigers. If you gave tigers your attention and respect, they would behave beautifully. But if you lost your concentration and turned your back on them, even for a moment, they would attack you. One trainer who got badly injured said afterward, "I deserved it—it was all my fault."

Sam put his fist behind his back. "Ellen," he said—and did his voice crack a bit?—"when is Barry's trial?"

I nearly groaned out loud. For a billion reasons this was my least favorite subject. "Barry's trial is scheduled for August," I said. Not for a whole entire month, I thought with relief.

"I'd like to attend," Sam said.

"Why?" I scrunched up my face. "What's it got to do with you?"

"I'm interested in—" Sam cut himself off.

"In what?"

"Nothing." He pulled at his gray T-shirt. He always wore gray, for some reason. "Just interested. Why, isn't Ray going with you?"

"Ray will be in Vermont," I said.

"What about that friend of yours?"

"Roz? She'll be up in Maine." My entire social life—leaving town for the summer. Anyway, I didn't want to tell Sam, but I wasn't going to attend Barry's trial either.

"I'd like to go," Sam said.

"Fine! You don't need my permission—a trial is open to the public. Go! Have a wonderful time! Send me a postcard!"

Maribeth came over to us. "Hello, young lovers! Could we close up shop now?"

Sam blushed a fiery red and again he took off. I was glad he left, if maybe a little sorry he got embarrassed. I can blush like that too, hot and vivid.

"Sam was asking about Barry's trial," I told Maribeth. "He wants to attend—I can't imagine why."

"He probably couldn't imagine your not wanting to. Sam would love to be able to point a finger at a doctor and say, That's him! That's the guy! He's the reason I have cerebral palsy."

"I shook my head. "I don't see why anybody needs to be blamed."

Gently Maribeth said, "That's very funny, especially coming from you."

Maribeth knew that for a long time I blamed myself for Barry's cerebral palsy. Way back, when I was eleven, and just starting to get good at things, wham!, my mother told me she was pregnant. This didn't fit into my plans at all. One middle-of-the-night I prayed to God that the baby would disappear. And then the baby was born—alive but damaged. For almost half a year I was convinced it was all my fault. "Don't you see?" I said to Maribeth now. "I don't need to blame anyone anymore."

"Honey, you're missing the point. Maybe something did go wrong, even if nobody wished it, and that's why Barry's not normal. And maybe this is the time to do something about it."

I looked down at the dark wood floor. It always came back to this. That *my* Barry was the wrong Barry. Would another Barry, a "normal" one, give the best hugs, holding tight to your neck and pressing his cheek against yours so you could feel his warm breath? This whole trial, which was open to anybody, even Sam, all centered around the imaginary Barry. And my Barry would have to be there in court, showing all those strangers how he wasn't as good as the other Barry.

"All right, all right." I held up my hands as if surrendering. "Let's say some doctor did something. Then everybody in the hospital could just go to the judge's office and tell him exactly what happened, and then the judge could decide what to do. Case closed."

Maribeth smoothed down some of the pleats in her dress. "That's not how it's done, honey. Everybody's got a version of the truth, and only a jury that's heard everybody's story can decide what really happened and what to do about it. So there will be a trial, Ellen, and it'll be long and messy and painful."

"Maybe that's why it appeals to Sam!" I said, sorry I'd said it out loud. Maribeth and Loretta were always telling me that Sam had changed, that a year of college had made him far less moody and sullen. Wishful thinking!

"What appeals to Sam," Maribeth said evenly, "is justice. Getting a jury to realize that a doctor was responsible for a child's disability, and awarding the child money. Sam was always frustrated that his cerebral palsy was caused by my contracting German measles in pregnancy. No justice and no money."

The money. What was Barry—a winning Lotto ticket? I've told my parents plenty of times not to worry, I thought. I'm going to take care of Barry—Barry's going to live with me, always. Case closed!

We turned off the lights, making a dark room even darker, and locked up. Outside, the air was close and sticky—you could taste the heat on your tongue. The light was a silver ghostly gray, and seemed to be coming up from below—I felt as if I was standing on it. For some reason I thought of Sam. What would he make of this unusual light? I practically had to grab my own shoulders and look myself in the eye. Sam had no right to be in my head. He couldn't just show up there the way he could at the trial.

two

That evening my best friend, Roz Spinak, came over, and we sprawled out with Loretta and Barry on the carpet of our living room and watched *The Wizard of Oz*. Behind the TV, the large windows of our loft let in lots of gray light. We live in Soho, a neighborhood just north of Tribeca.

"Bird-monkeys!" Barry cried out with affection, pointing at the flying, grinning monkeys. His voice is thick and nasal. Barry rarely speaks in front of strangers, but when he does, people turn to gaze at him with utter blankness. You can feel them thinking, Those are *words*?

"I'm glad you're not scared of the monkeys," I said.

"Monkeys, my favorite, Nellie," Barry said, his light blue eyes open wide. He always calls me Nellie. "And the big green city."

"Oz," I said.

The Wizard of Oz was Roz's, and Barry's, all-time favorite movie. "You can learn so much from it, Ellie," Roz once said. "But you have to *listen* and *watch*." So what else do you do with a movie?

"See, Ellie, the Wicked Witch of the West really has no power," Roz was telling me now. "Look, she's got Dorothy in her castle, the ruby slippers are right at her fingertips—and what happens? She turns an hourglass upside down and leaves the room!"

"I never thought of that," Loretta said. She'd braided her light-blond hair and was wearing bleached shorts and a big T-shirt. She looked like a little kid staring up at a movie. "The Wicked Witch always terrified me so much, it never occurred to me she was powerless."

"At the end she's killed by water," Roz said. "Plain, ordinary water!"

I hadn't studied the movie as if it were a chemistry final, but it seemed to me the Wicked Witch had power, loads of it. "Haven't we seen her throwing a fireball at the scarecrow?" I asked. "Don't tell me she was hiding it up her sleeve."

Roz smoothed her short black hair back behind her ears. A few years before, her large jaw and puffy cheeks had made her appear awkward, but now, at seventeen, Roz is very beautiful. Her best features are her glowing skin and her light brown, almond-shaped eyes. In school Roz is a year ahead of me. She'd be entering college in September, studying to be a cartoonist—the Rhode Island School of Design, which she calls "Rizdee." This summer she was off to teach at an art camp. "The fireball?" Roz said. "So she's learned a few tricks."

"What'd she do, take a class for ugly green witches?"

"Ellie, I'm trying to educate you! There are people in this world exactly like the Wicked Witch of the West—people with no power who will try to psyche you out."

"Don't worry about me," I said. "I know exactly who they are, and can spot 'em a mile away." I was thinking of Aunt Beryl, Loretta's older sister, who used to be able to upset me terribly and occasionally still gave it the old college try. Aunt Beryl disapproved of Barry's trial, for reasons of her own. One of her scenarios had the doctor we were suing getting so mad he'd turn around and sue us back, leaving us emotionally and financially ruined. "This trial will destroy your family," Aunt Beryl predicted.

"Maybe there are a few wicked witches you haven't met yet," Roz told me ominously.

I squished my fingers into the carpet. It's extra thick, and all our furniture is heavily upholstered and marshmallow soft because Barry's balance is so poor. "Roz," I said, "you've watched this movie too many times."

"You can't see it too many times. You always find something different, something new."

"I used to dislike Auntie Em," Loretta said. "I thought she neglected Dorothy. Now I just feel sorry for her, and I think she really loves Dorothy after all." Loretta's gray-blue eyes looked a little sad.

"Now, see, Dorothy has power," Roz went on. "But she won't realize it until after the end. She thought she was just Dorothy, the small and meek, but she's really the Good Witch of the South."

"Roz, when the movie's over, it's over! Dorothy doesn't realize anything!"

"Roz, Oz," Barry said, laughing. "Roz, Oz!"

Roz leaned over to hug Barry. "What a terrific poem,"

she said. "Maybe Barry will be a poet, and live out in the country somewhere, to be alone with his thoughts. Mmm, Barry, you smell so good, like shampoo and pineapple."

Roz knew Barry was going to live with me, but always imagined him off by himself somewhere. Once we were with Barry in Cave, standing before a painting of a tree-smothered mountain at sunset. Barry said something like "The painting is breathing." Roz got all excited. "He knows," she said to me. "The painting is alive. He should go to Paris, study the light, get some training. He could become an artist." *With cerebral palsy?* I had to explain that Barry had trouble with his perceptions, that he might actually see the painting inhaling and exhaling. It didn't make a dent. Roz said van Gogh had epilepsy. She said Goya had lead poisoning that brought on hallucinations. She said that for handicapped kids doors were always closing, so you constantly had to open the other doors—invent them, if necessary.

The phone rang and Loretta went to the kitchen to answer it.

"I love the music," Roz said as the credits came on. "'Somewhere Over the Rainbow'—that song makes you happy to cry."

So the three of us sat there and listened, and I thought, This is a good moment.

When Loretta came back, right away I knew something had happened. Her whole body looked agitated, as if she'd just seen a car wreck.

I swallowed hard. "Mom—is Daddy okay?" I hadn't called him that in years.

"Daddy?" Loretta said. "Daddy's fine. That wasn't about Daddy. It wasn't about anybody—I mean, you know, about anybody we know, in terms of are they okay or not okay."

Rambling was not Loretta's usual style of conversation.

"Would you like to sit down?" Roz said.

"Yes," she said, but still she stood there. I wished she hadn't braided her hair; she looked as lost as Dorothy caught up in the twister. "El, they called."

"They"—it came out sounding like a scary movie from the 1950s about giant ants. But I knew who she meant. "It's the law firm representing Barry's case," I said, for Roz's benefit. "So, what did they want?"

"Our lawyer is coming over first thing Monday morning, before work. El, the trial isn't supposed to start for a month. Why are they calling now, on a Saturday night? Robert's halfway around the world! What if the trial's been pushed up?"

"Mom, wait till Monday morning, wait to see what the lawyer wants." It made me shudder, just knowing that the lawyer was coming here, to our loft. I'd always thought medical-malpractice lawyers were sleazy, the lowest of the low, the substitute teachers of the legal profession.

Barry pulled at the Velcro on his knee pads.

"I'll have to call Claire," Loretta said.

Claire was Claire Withers Stonehill, Barry's therapist. She works with Barry every day after school, from two o'clock to six o'clock. "Why Claire?" I asked.

"She was thinking of taking a vacation soon. I have to warn her that the trial might be starting."

"You don't know that," I said as gently as I could. "Besides, what's the trial got to do with Claire?"

Loretta said matter-of-factly, "Claire offered to testify."

"What!" Now it was my turn to stand up. Claire Withers Stonehill was a totally separate part of Barry's life. She wasn't supposed to spill over into the trial. "Why is she doing that?"

"She's an expert on Barry," Loretta explained.

"So am I!" I said, my insides tightening. There was a time, when Barry was about a year old, when I wouldn't let anyone near him, not even my mother. Only I knew who Barry was, what he needed. This trial—I could feel it pulling me backward and under, like a powerfully strong undertow.

"Of course you're an expert," Loretta said. "Far more than Claire is, as she'd be the first to agree. But I thought you didn't want anything to do with Barry's case."

"No, I didn't. I mean, I don't."

Now Roz gave me a look. I knew she disapproved. She thought I should be submerged in the trial—probably prosecute the doctor myself.

"So, there you are," Loretta said.

"Where?" Barry said, kidding around, covering his eyes. "Where is Nellie?"

"Right here," I replied, but my voice sounded far away from itself.

When Roz said good-bye that night, she told me, "Don't forget, you promised to write twice a week. Last summer all I got was two lousy postcards with the same unflattering picture of the Statue of Liberty. And don't forget, you promised to visit my dad."

"I'll miss you," I said.

"About Barry's case—" Roz began.

"I know," I cut her off. "Listen, I'll try."

She gave me a sideways smile. "Try what?"

"Try to be part of the trial, somehow."

The spectacular gray light was gone, and it was just plain old dark.

three

The doorbell woke me Monday morning. I had just decided to lie in bed and wait until the lawyer said what he had to say and left, when I realized I was starving. I hardly cared that I was wearing only a knee-length T-shirt and my hair was sticking straight up as if I'd stuck my finger in a socket. All I could think about was a toasted onion bagel with fresh mozzarella and anchovies. Heaven.

In the narrow hall between my room and the kitchen, I caught a glimpse of Loretta holding Barry. Her hair was up on top of her head, and she wore a tan linen suit. She could wear jeans to work—this was for the lawyer. "Good morning, El!" she called. "He's on his way upstairs."

So why did I stand in the hall and stare ahead at the front door? Maybe I was morbidly curious to see an actual medical-malpractice lawyer—like wanting to know, while not wanting to know, what was beneath an eye patch.

Tall, he was, and very thin, almost giving the appearance of walking on low stilts. He had short, close, frizzy hair, like a bathing cap made of brown Brillo, high cheekbones, a long jaw, and an emphasized eyebrow ridge with thick, bushy eyebrows. He wore a muted blue suit that looked expensive; the material didn't shine but seemed to glow with light. A thin belt wrapped halfway again around his narrow waist. I couldn't begin to guess his age—an old-looking thirty-five? A young sixty?

"Ellen, come meet Jack Frazier."

Jack Frazier. I liked his name, at least—it was good and strong, a name you could bite into like a tart apple. As I got closer, I saw that Jack Frazier was far from classically good-looking. But his eyes were spectacular, brown with tiny flecks of green. Jack Frazier shook my hand. He smelled like the middle of a forest.

"Lovely to meet you, Elena," Jack Frazier said, and smiled a wide-open smile.

Elena, he had called me.

"Her name is Ellen," Loretta said with emphasis.

"No!" I said, a bit louder than I'd intended. "It's okay, how he said it."

Jack Frazier laughed. "Right, then. Elena, it is."

"Elena" should be a stunning girl in a black dress with mysterious eyes and dark curls tumbling down her back. But there I was, my hair measuring 7.5 on the Richter scale, wearing a T-shirt that said, I'M HAVING A NEAR-DEATH EXPERIENCE. Ray had gotten it for my sixteenth birthday. What a dumb gift, it occurred to me now, though I'd liked it then.

"Hello, little fellow," Jack Frazier said to Barry. "How are you doing?"

"Fine, thank you," Barry said.

"He answered you!" Loretta said with a laugh. "Usually Barry won't talk to people he doesn't know."

We all sat down in the living room—Loretta and Barry on the couch, and Jack Frazier and I in easy chairs on either side. Warm air swirled through our open windows; the bakery downstairs sent up the aroma of fruit-filled doughnuts, the squishy kind. "So, do you like school?" Jack Frazier asked Barry.

Barry smiled and shrugged, then looked to me.

"Go on," I urged him. I put my index finger to the side of one nostril and twisted my finger, which in Sign language means "boring." Then I took my index and middle fingers and stroked the tip of my nose, twice—the sign for "fun."

Barry laughed and said, "Both—boring and fun!"

"What was that?" Jack Frazier said.

"Ask Ellen," Loretta said. "She's the only one who understands Barry all the time."

Roz would like this, I thought. My chatting away with the lawyer, translating what Barry just said, joining in the spirit of things. "About a year ago," I explained, "Barry's teacher at UCP taught him some Sign language so he'd feel more confident about being understood in class. When he signs at home, we're all supposed to make sure Barry says words as he does it. Signing isn't meant to replace spoken language, but to help it along."

Jack Frazier's brown-green eyes were fixed on me. If I didn't know better, I'd think I was dazzling him with my brilliant remarks. "You have great empathy and understanding for your brother, don't you?" Jack Frazier said. "And you get along well. I like that."

Just then I noticed the accent. A slight drawl on the "l" in "like," and a clipping off of the words "get" and "that." Also, the emphasis wasn't exactly American, somehow. "You have an accent," I said.

"Indeed I do," Jack Frazier said. "Not a bad thing for a trial lawyer to have. A little attention-getting device for the jury."

I said, "Like an eye patch."

Jack Frazier laughed a deep, throaty laugh. "An eye patch is perfect. A wooden leg's not bad, either."

"But where are you from?" I asked.

"Born in Ireland, but I've lived all over the world, and everywhere I lived I stole a piece of the accent."

So that was it. He had the accent of a thousand places, and no place.

"My mother was a nightclub singer," he said. "Whenever a job beckoned, we picked up and left, even if it meant moving to a brand-new country."

"What an exotic life!" I sighed. We'd only lived in New York City, and in Connecticut when I was very young. Basically all I can remember is *here*.

"I suppose it sounds exotic, but it didn't feel that way. Sometimes all I had to eat for a week was one egg. But we lived by our wits, and got by."

"And grew up to become a brilliant trial lawyer," Loretta said. "A year ago Ms. Hoffman told me after my EBT that I'd be lucky to get you."

EBT—Examination Before Trial. It was a kind of trial-before-the-trial, where my parents answered question after question under oath, questions asked by lawyers from both sides.

"Ms. Hoffman is extremely flattering," Jack Frazier said.

A totally self-made man, and modest about it, too. I kept waiting for him to display his ambulance-chaser tendencies, but he wasn't doing it.

"Mrs. Gray." He took a deep breath. "You've probably figured out why I've come to see you. I know your husband is away, but Barry's case has been calendared for this week. I'm truly sorry." He did sound genuinely sorry. "Sometimes the trial gets pushed back six months, and sometimes it happens this way, when suddenly it's upon you."

Loretta smoothed down Barry's brown hair, but he pushed her hand away. "I can't call my husband and tell him to hurry home," she said. "We can write these telegrams, you see—they're called familygrams—but they're heavily censored and we're not supposed to send along any worrisome news. If he knew the trial was proceeding without him, he'd feel just terrible, and helpless to do anything about it."

"Your husband was away for Barry's birth and for much of Barry's infancy," Jack Frazier said. "His EBT was only thirty-five pages. Yours was over two hundred. Your testimony will be sufficient." He held out his hands as if offering an invisible basket. "Mrs. Gray, this won't hurt our case. I'll simply tell the jury that your husband is serving our country, defending it against all enemies—no doubt they'll be most impressed."

Loretta said quietly, "But I'll be alone."

"No," Jack Frazier said firmly. "I'll be there."

"Me, too," I broke in. "I'll be there, too."

Loretta looked at me, unblinking.

"I'll sit beside my mother in the courtroom," I told Jack Frazier. "Plus I'd like to testify, too."

"You're kidding!" Loretta said. "Ellen, you've always—"

"I want to testify," I interrupted her.

Jack Frazier rubbed his chin and looked at me even longer and harder than before. I could feel the intensity of his gaze, as if it were bright light. "It's always a judgment call, whether to use the sibling," he said. "The defense lawyer might argue that any child born to these parents would be brain damaged. But there you are—attractive, intelligent, articulate—showing the jury that your parents can produce a normal child."

I basked in the glow of his compliments. Jack Frazier could see beyond the juvenile T-shirt and the unruly hair. He saw me as attractive, intelligent, articulate, and, I guessed, most important of all—normal.

"Are you sure about this?" Loretta said, and again I told her yes. I wished she'd stop sounding so incredulous!

Jack Frazier's attention was still totally on me: "You've got to be on time every morning, and back in court on time after every lunch. There's nothing worse than a jury looking for you and seeing an empty seat. You're not to talk or fidget or chew gum or laugh or cry. You've got to look like the sister of a handicapped child."

But how do you look like that?

"Beware of your demeanor and appearance," I heard Jack Frazier say.

"Beware?" I asked. "Why beware?"

"Be aware," he said carefully. "Dress conservatively, in simple blouses, skirts, dresses, sensible shoes." How perfect! He was practically looking in my closet. "God help you if I see basketball sneakers or dangling earrings or micro-miniskirts—or T-shirts with writing splashed all over them."

"I never wear those!" And I blushed, hot and vivid. "Not out of the house, I mean."

"And not a hint of cleavage," Jack Frazier warned me.

The blush only got worse. I had a sudden image of Jack Frazier—long legs crossed, leaning back on my bed, green-and-brown eyes fully on me. I was trying on outfits for him, putting clothes on, taking clothes off.

Jack Frazier clasped his hands tight and the image dissolved. "This is your brother's only chance at justice," he said to me. "Do you understand? His only chance."

I clasped my hands too, to show him I understood.

"Right, then," he said. "Elena, you're in."

I was in! I was Elena! The phone rang, and in a rush of excitement I ran to answer it. It was Aunt Beryl. "Can't talk," I told her. "My lawyer is here—I mean, Barry's lawyer, and the case is starting this week—" Aunt Beryl told me to slow down. She said I was wrong. She insisted the case wasn't coming up until August. "It's changed," I said. "Everything's all different now." And I said proudly, "I'm going to testify!" When I got back to the living room, I said, "That was Aunt Beryl. I told her we were busy, with the trial starting up and everything."

Loretta's expression grew still. Something occurred to her, I could see it, but then she pushed the thought away.

Jack Frazier didn't notice. "I'll be selecting a jury, starting tomorrow," he told her.

"Can't we see that?" I blurted out.

He paused. "I strongly discourage the family from attending the *voir dire*. I must explain a rather complicated case and pose many questions to several different batches of prospective jurors—it can take days. There are plenty of people out there who greatly resent lawsuits against doctors, and it takes a while for them to admit their biases. They'll be more open and honest if the family suing the doctor isn't staring right at them." Maybe I looked disappointed, because he added, "Even the judge won't be present."

I nodded. "Right. We won't be there."

Jack Frazier nodded back. Then a strange thing happened. Something seemed to click off inside him—his attention, as if it needed to be elsewhere. He was out the door before he'd even left the room. "I'll call to let you know when your part in the trial will begin," said the person who was there and not-there. "Be ready anytime."

I watched Jack Frazier turn and actually go out the door; I heard his footsteps go down three flights of stairs. Now he was gone, but that was strange, too, because part of him remained in the room, like an afterimage, an optical illusion.

Loretta said, "El, what happened? You floored me!"

I shrugged. "Nothing happened. Roz thinks it's a good idea. Sam mentioned he wanted to go. That got me thinking I might want to go too."

She was shaking her head. "Something pushed you over the top, made you want to testify. What really changed your mind?"

How could I explain it to her when I could barely explain it to myself? "Mom," I said, "how old is Jack Frazier?"

"About forty-five," she said. "El, I just want to make sure you're not doing something you don't want to do because you're concerned about me."

"So he's older than Dad." My father was forty-two. It bothered me a little, that I'd had such thoughts about a man older than Robert. Was Jack Frazier married? He didn't wear a ring. And he didn't *seem* married. I could almost picture him eating dinner in a restaurant every night, table for one.

"*El*," Loretta said.

"What? Oh, no, I want to be there. It'll be fascinating to be part of the trial and send the doctor to jail."

"Jail!" Barry said, all excited. "Wicked witches go to jail."

Loretta laughed. "Maybe wicked witches do, but doctors don't. Medical malpractice cases aren't criminal, and only criminals go to jail."

"Why?" I said.

"It's a question of intent. No doctor sets out to harm a child. That would be criminal, not to mention crazy! Medical malpractice cases are only about damages and who has to pay for them. In this case, the damage is Barry's cerebral palsy."

"So if he doesn't go to jail, will he lose all his money?"

"No, his insurance company pays out."

I remembered that about three months before, Loretta had rejected an offer from the insurance company to settle for one hundred and fifty thousand dollars. I also remembered feeling frustrated that Loretta didn't simply take the money and end the case before it even began. Now I was glad she hadn't settled. "Of course, the doctor will lose his job," I said.

She shook her head.

"I don't understand. It sounds like the doctor, guilty or not, gets away with everything."

"Maybe not everything. His insurance premiums might go up, and the trial itself is very stressful. The hope is that the doctor will be more careful in the future."

I frowned. "It doesn't sound like much, for causing cerebral palsy."

Loretta smiled. "Punishing the doctor is not our number one concern, Ellen. All we're trying to do is prove that this doctor did not do what any good doctor should have done in the same circumstances. The courts protect good, careful doctors who are sometimes sued falsely or frivolously. If they've done everything they should have done, any lawsuit against them probably won't get very far."

A fire engine wailed by, setting off a few car alarms. I realized I wasn't hungry anymore. Where did the hunger go? Something had replaced it. Something more filling than food.

four

Our dates were always a threesome—me, Ray Frost, and the clipboard. Ray wanted to be a science-fiction writer, and he was constantly taking notes on a novel that was "so long," as he liked to say, "by the time people reach the end they'll have forgotten the beginning—so they'll have to read it all over again." He said this would make it the perfect book, the only book anybody would ever need.

Thursday, the third of July, the night before Ray was leaving for a summer in Vermont with his mother and identical twin brother, Bob, we took a long walk on Bleecker Street. The book, seven hundred pages and counting, but still untitled, seemed to have more subplots than characters. And Ray was telling me about yet another one.

"There's an actor who's determined to take on the lead in the legendary play about hypnosis, *Your Eyes Are*

Getting Heavy." Ray checked off something on the clipboard. "But no one's produced this play in twenty years. Want to know why? Because for twenty years no one has dared to play the lead. Want to know why?" Ray lowered his voice to a whisper. "Because after opening night the star always goes insane."

We passed a sidewalk café where people were gesturing across large bowls of pasta; one couple seemed lost in each other's words. I could hear fireworks, probably over in Washington Square. "Ray, how can an actor go insane playing a role?"

"It's something about the words he has to say and the moods they conjure up."

"But hasn't the actor rehearsed it over and over? And dress rehearsals are practically like opening nights."

"Yes, and previews are even more so. But there's something about opening night. It's really real; it's more real than real; it's so real that it feels like it can't possibly be real. That's one of my themes." Ray flipped back his long, wavy blond hair. He'd stopped cutting it two years before, around the time we started going out. "Are you hungry?"

"Not yet." Not since Jack Frazier's visit, to be exact. Jack Frazier was so thin. He had a real runner's body—long, lean. I could see him in a tank top and bicycle shorts, legs graceful and fast. . . . I cleared my throat. "Ray, how about an understudy?"

Ray stopped walking and kissed me. I could feel the clipboard press into my chest. "Ellen! An understudy! He'd be quite a fascinating person, don't you think? Yearning to perform, yet terrified to perform?" He scribbled this down. "Now, I wanted to ask you. My actor is going to beat the system. He's going to perform opening night, and night after night, and not go insane."

"How?"

Ray blinked at me. "I was hoping you'd know."

I sighed.

Ray crossed something out and we walked on. At a haircutting place, people emerged with short buzz cuts like freshly cut grass. "I was trying to think of things kids in the future could do to shock their parents," he said. "So far I came up with braided underarm hair."

I laughed. "That's disgusting! How about . . . blackened teeth?"

"Not bad!" Ray wrote it down.

"Panty hose that look like you have varicose veins."

"Ellen, you're a genius. I can call them 'Very Vari.'"

"Or 'Very Veiny—in vari-ous colors.' Ray, how will you get along without me this summer?"

"I can mail you my questions."

"Thanks a lot! I didn't know I had to go to summer school this year."

Ray stopped walking right next to a man holding open a briefcase full of suspiciously cheap gold watches. "I love you madly and this summer will be intolerable without you."

"Rolex for the lady?" the man said. "Ten bucks."

They were both waiting for me to say something. "No, thank you," I said to the man, but I was looking at Ray. Ray's eyes are green and close set together.

"Ellen, I mean it," he said.

Just then I heard a familiar, cheerful, singsong voice behind me: "Ellen! Ray!" It was Susie Brockleman, walking her big white standard poodle, Misty. I've known Susie since first grade, and even then her top priorities were pleasing boys and pleasing teachers. She'd cut off all her dark curls and bobbed her hair. "How's your father?" she asked me. "I thought maybe he'd quit his submarine job, with the Cold War over and everything." She nodded at Ray. "Oh, hi, Ray."

"Hi," he responded.

"My father's on patrol," I said. "The Cold War may be over, but the world will always be restless."

"He's not in the Soviet Union, is he?" It sounded as if the Soviet Union, which didn't even exist anymore, still scared her.

"He's on something called a Med run—a routine ride through the Mediterranean Sea." In the days of tighter security, I'd never have even known where Robert was.

Susie ran her fingers through a big ball of fur on Misty's head. "The Mediterranean—how romantic."

"Susie, not three hundred feet beneath it!" I said. "It's not exactly Club Med!"

"I know," Susie said, and shook her hair. "Anyway, when he comes back, tell him I hope he had a wonderful trip." She turned to Ray and asked politely, "Are you enjoying your summer?"

"So far, so good," he said. "And you?" Susie and Ray had gone out for a while, but you'd think they hadn't even met yet.

"You won't forget?" Susie asked me in a small voice, before turning to go. "You'll mention me, and what I said?"

I nodded. I'd told Robert that Susie Brockleman had a crush on him, and he'd said, "She's just a little girl. It's harmless enough." She'd have been devastated to hear that. It made me almost sorry for her.

On the corner, there was a display of incense—long, thin, upright sticks sending streams of powerfully scented smoke into the air. It smelled like a nightclub in a far-off place. I could almost see Jack Frazier as a little kid, backstage, listening to his mother sing. Ray grabbed hold of my arm and we started walking again. It didn't matter that Ray and I would be apart all summer. We'd simply pick up exactly where we left off, like a carousel that coasts to a stop and then glides around once more. Roz never understood that Ray—low-key, nice, steady—was the perfect boyfriend for me. He didn't clutter up my head.

So why did I ask Ray, out of nowhere, "Do you love Barry?"

Ray looked a little taken aback. "Barry—your brother, Barry? Sure, he's a cute kid."

"Could you love him like a son?" I asked.

"Ellen, he's your brother!"

Jack Frazier would love him like that, I thought. And felt like shaking myself all over, as if I were a soaking-wet standard poodle. Susie Brockleman got crushes on older men, not me!

"I have a going-away present for you," I told Ray. "Since your play is about hypnosis, why not have your actor perform his role while under hypnosis? He can go out on opening night thinking it's just another dress rehearsal."

Ray seemed to be thinking this over. "Not bad, Ellen."

"Ray, I'm going to testify at Barry's trial."

"Great!" he replied. "Let me know if you get stage fright. I can use a good description. Let me know if you stutter, like that time in seventh grade, in Ms. Stapler's speech class."

"That was long, long ago, and entirely different," I said. "I won't stutter—unless Ms. Stapler herself shows up in court."

Just ahead of us a dark-eyed woman in a kerchief, sitting behind a card table, flipped tarot cards for a girl about my age. The woman glanced up and gave me a challenging look. But I would never have my fortune told. It would be like hearing the end of a movie you'd been dying to see.

When I got home, Barry was already asleep, and Loretta sat at the kitchen table, filling out stacks of insurance forms for him. Barry's school, United Cerebral Palsy, was free, and therapy with Claire was covered by the Navy's insurance company, CHAMPUS. But public school ended with high school, and CHAMPUS covered Barry's care only until Robert retired. That was when I would come in—grab the baton and run with it.

"How'd it go?" Loretta asked me, stretching her back. Probably she'd been leaning over the table for hours.

"Fine," I said, as if talking about a test.

"Jack Frazier called," Loretta said simply.

"Oh—I'm sorry I missed that."

"It was a ten-second phone call, Ellen. He wanted us to know it took him three and a half days to select a jury. Tomorrow's a holiday, so the trial will begin Monday, nine thirty sharp, down at Sixty Centre Street."

I got a strange feeling—my real life was about to begin, Monday, nine thirty sharp, down at Sixty Centre Street.

The night before the trial, we had hours of heat lighting. The sky lit up like the flashbulbs of old-time cameras; there were spider bursts of light, and jagged bolts, and double bolts, and grumbly rumblings that sounded as if the bright, restless sky was enormously hungry.

Loretta and I sat by our windows and looked out at the light show that was more dramatic than any Fourth of July fireworks could ever be.

"I was thinking about something I heard in my parents' group," Loretta said. "One of the fathers said that having a child with a disability is like living with a rock 'n' roll station blaring in your head, nonstop, twenty-four hours a day. I know what he means. There's a kind of noise that doesn't die down or go away. But tonight I feel quiet, peaceful. I wondered if I'd have any second thoughts or misgivings about the trial, but I don't. And I'm so glad you'll be there, El. I'm only sorry that by the time Robert comes home, the trial will probably be over."

"We'll have good news for him, Mom. We'll win Barry's case—you, me, and Jack Frazier."

double setup

five

First thing every morning: turning off my bedside lamp in the shape of a duck. Loretta always teased me about sleeping with a light on at my age, but the way I saw it, who needs utter darkness? This morning, though, the first day of the trial, I left it on, because pale yellow light was shining directly on Barry, curled up in his blue pajamas at the foot of my bed. He'd wandered into my room before, during the night, but only a couple of times.

Did Barry understand about the trial? *This trial is all about you*, Loretta had told Barry. *Many people, including Mommy and Ellen, will go to a big building every day and listen to a lot of questions, all about you.*

A big building, he'd said. *Full of questions.*

Claire will pick you up after school and stay with you until we come home. Barry, you'll go to the room too, but only once, and maybe answer a question or two yourself.

Barry opened his eyes. Sky blue, their color, though usually the sky wasn't nearly so light and sharp and clear. "Barry, don't you worry," I told him. "No matter what, Nellie will always take care of you."

Barry rolled around on the bed, humming loudly.

Loretta, wet from a shower and wrapped in a bathrobe, appeared in my doorway. "Good, you're both awake," she said. "El, up or down? My hair."

I loved her hair, yellow as light. "Down," I said.

Loretta frowned at me. "I thought up. More businesslike."

"So, go ahead—up."

"But if you really think down . . ."

Barry laughed. "Elevators go up and down."

"That's right!" I said. "Very good, Barry. Mom, are you nervous?" Would Loretta have curled up on my bed too, if there was room?

Loretta laughed—a nervous laugh. "I didn't think so," she said. "I mean, I picked out an outfit: my tan linen suit, tan shoes. But what about my hair? My mind just fell apart over a stupid little thing!"

"Wear it up," I told her.

Loretta let out a deep breath. "Thank you, Ellen," she said, as if I'd told her her destiny and it had satisfied her.

Barry went off for breakfast with Loretta as I stared at the clothes in my closet. My short-sleeved white blouse looked electrically white—there could have been batteries inside the sleeves. My navy-blue cotton skirt, the one that fell a respectable distance below my knees, looked as austere as a nun's habit. This was my outfit, all right, practically leaping out at me.

I looked in the mirror over my bureau more closely

than I had in months, hearing Jack Frazier's voice in my head: *You've got to look like the sister of a handicapped child.* And it hit me—for this trial, that was all I was supposed to be. Not somebody who liked somber paintings, or who had Roz Spinak for a best friend, or who craved onion bagels with mozzarella cheese and anchovies. I had to become a fraction of my self: dress like a fraction, act like a fraction, and, when I testified, talk like a fraction.

Meet Ellen Gray. Part of me, anyway.

I still had no appetite, and skipped breakfast altogether. My stomach, at least, had already become a fraction.

Loretta and I walked Barry downstairs in time for his bus from United Cerebral Palsy, which stops right at our corner. Then we walked the half mile or so to the courthouse, and I noticed that in her tan suit, hair up, she looked older. Loretta, who could still look like a kid whenever she felt like it, was clearly now "the mother of a handicapped child." We walked quietly beneath blotchy clouds, two fractions side by side. Together did we add up to even one whole person?

The courthouse sat at the top of wide, gray steps, behind tall stone columns. And inside, instead of the dark, crumbling mess I'd expected, it was gorgeous. It's a six-sided building with a rotunda in the middle, like a nut wrapped around a bolt. Within the rotunda, a huge starburst covered the marble floor—I could hear heels clicking on it, people moving swiftly, urgently. The walls were covered with color-soaked murals of colonial life in old New York.

"It's like a museum," I whispered to Loretta, so that two men nearby holding briefcases that looked like bulging accordions couldn't hear.

"It's elegant on purpose," Loretta whispered back, "to demonstrate the majesty of the law."

No, I thought, it's to make you feel like a stranger, only blocks from your own home.

We got off at the fourth floor and walked halfway around the circle that was the hall along the outer edge of the rotunda. I'd never been in a circular hall before—it felt one degree off from normal, like a round refrigerator. High swinging doors, Old West style, led to a large, quiet room that was all oak and light. IN GOD WE TRUST was painted in tall letters high up on the front wall; beneath the words sat the judge at her huge oak desk, next to a large flagpole with a streamlined eagle on top. Everything felt big and permanent and ancient, as if a glacier had dumped it all here during the last ice age. It even smelled clean and sharp, like ice.

The judge was an elegant African-American woman. Her dark hair was pulled back, exposing a high, smooth forehead; she had large brown eyes behind gold-rimmed glasses, and she wore a black robe. Loretta walked over to her, and got a smile and a handshake; they exchanged a few words, and then Loretta came back.

"Judge Patterson said there's been a delay," Loretta said.

"Delay?" I said. "How long?" A delay sounded so empty, open-ended. I always got edgy when movies failed to start exactly on time.

"Judge Patterson didn't say," Loretta told me. "She seems like an extraordinary woman."

The fraction, I thought, or the whole person?

Next to Judge Patterson was the witness stand (a chair, really); on one adjoining wall were two rows of padded swivel seats for the jury, and windows half-covered by yellow shades. An oak banister separated the jury seats from the spectator seats—six oak benches, three on each side of an aisle, that could each hold about four people. On the back wall was a big clock with a second hand that staggered around as if hopelessly confused. Four thirty, the clock said—about five hours off. An air conditioner hummed and worked a little too well—my arms got goose bumps.

One person sat in the back row, quietly reading a paper. Sam, in a light gray suit.

"I don't want to sit with Sam," I whispered to Loretta automatically. But something in me did want to.

"We have to sit up front," Loretta said, indicating the bench closest to the jury. "But you can at least say hello."

"No thanks!" I said, again on automatic.

Loretta shrugged at me and went off to talk to Sam.

Just then a redheaded man in uniform—blue pants, a white shirt, and a shiny badge—came up to me and demanded, "Are you the judge? Do we have a verdict?"

I just stared at him. "Am I—what?" I noticed he had a gun. Awkwardly I gestured toward Judge Patterson.

"You looked so somber, I had to do something!" He laughed.

I smiled—or tried to, anyway.

"I'm the court officer," he said. And told me his name, which I couldn't grasp.

"Hans?" I said. "Hansel?"

"Everyone gets it wrong," he explained. "Hannes." Pronounced hah-ness. "It's short for Johannes—the Austrian version of John. Hannes Leeser."

"I'm Ellen Gray," I said, and we shook hands. His

handshake was gentle, especially for somebody with a gun.

"See that guy coming in to fix the clock?" Hannes Leeser pointed to a man holding a large ladder. "Twelve years ago his wife went in for a hernia operation. Doctor left her in a coma. Jack Frazier got him twenty million dollars."

"Twenty million dollars!" I breathed out.

"Hannes, stop it!" said a woman with long, frizzy black hair. "Stop waving the millions around!" She also wore blue pants, a white shirt, and a silver badge, but to jazz it all up she wore large hoop earrings and a couple dozen shiny bracelets. "Exciting things don't happen in this room too often. Hannes and I see a lot of medical mal, and I have to tell you, the doctor usually wins. How many times does the patient win? Only one out of five. And how much money does he usually win? Two thousand dollars or less."

"But her lawyer is Jack Frazier," Hannes said proudly. "His win percentage is better than anybody's."

"You and your Jack Frazier!" the woman went on. "Your idol can do no wrong. But like any good lawyer, he wins and he loses."

"Don't listen to Sheila," Hannes Leeser said. "Jack Frazier hasn't lost a case in three years."

"Don't you go getting her hopes way up high," Sheila said. "The odds of a million-dollar verdict are barely one in a thousand."

I felt as if I were in Las Vegas instead of in the Supreme Court of New York.

A phone rang at the desk on the other side of the room, opposite the jurors. Sheila went to answer it, and I noticed she had a spectacular figure, real 1950s hourglass glamour. "Natalie?" she said. "Make sure Marlene eats her breakfast." It was the exact same tone of voice she'd taken with me.

The twenty-million-dollar man had fixed the clock: It was nine thirty-five. Jack Frazier breezed in, and I couldn't believe the accusing tone in my voice as I said, "What happened to nine thirty sharp!"

But Jack Frazier gave me a friendly smile. "I was here at eight o'clock sharp." He emphasized the *sharp*. "I knew all about the delay. Elena, you look just perfect."

I gave him a friendly smile back.

So I sat on my bench as the oak doors to the courtroom kept swinging open and swinging shut, while men and women in suits hurried in, spoke to the judge, and left. Absolutely nothing was going on to indicate that an actual trial was about to start. I asked Hannes Leeser how long this delay would last, and he said he had no idea.

"The judge has business," he said, "paperwork, procedures, past cases, cases coming up. We could wait a few more minutes or a few more hours."

"A few more *hours*?" What was I going to do with myself?

But the time passed. A short, pale man with curly brown hair sat down and flipped through papers at an oak table in front of the benches on the other side of the courtroom.

"Elena," Jack Frazier leaned down to whisper in my ear, "don't talk to that man, ever. Come to me immediately if he so much as taps you on the shoulder." I felt like I was four years old, getting lectured on strangers offering candy. "That's Charles Friss, the doctor's lawyer, and you're to stay away from him and everyone else connected to the doctor. They'll always sit over there–that's the other side, literally and figuratively. The enemy side."

Enemy? I said, "Mr. Frazier—"

"Jack," he interrupted me.

"Okay–Jack." This felt a little . . . intimate, somehow. It's only a name, I had to tell myself. "What's your win percentage?"

He laughed. "You've been talking to Hannes Leeser, have you? I'm happy to say it's about ninety percent. I've had forty verdicts over a million dollars, including ten verdicts over ten million." I must have been gaping at him, because he remarked, "I'll take that expression as a compliment."

Hannes Leeser told me not to stray too far or for too long from the courtroom. "That's how it'll all begin–suddenly," he said. "It'll end that way, too."

So I only went to the ladies' room. Actually, on the fourth floor there was no ladies' room. A sign that said LADIES ROOM led to a flight of stairs, at the top of which was a men's room, with MEN crossed out and *Ladies* scrawled in red Magic Marker. It was unbelievably gloomy: a row of urinals, four stalls with broken doors off their hinges, and no mirrors. It was like a bathroom in a bad dream.

Waiting, waiting, waiting.

Loretta chatted away with Sheila as if they'd been buddies since high school. Sam read every single word in that newspaper. Sam was a terrific reader: according to Maribeth, he could go through three books a day. "People see him walking funny and assume he's retarded, too," she said. "They don't have your X-ray vision, Ellen. As the sister of a handicapped child, you can see beyond the outside into the inside." But I'd never wanted to see the inside of Sam. What would I find there? A *No Trespassing* sign, probably.

Hannes Leeser told me about the jury. "There's always a whiner," he said, "but mostly they're pretty nice—and smart, too. You want smart, because in cases like this you have to think." He tapped my forehead, telling me I had to think too. "We've got a guy who works in a bank, and an actress, and a lady who works in a department store, and an electrician, and an office manager, and a lady in publishing, and a retired lady who used to design clothes, and a young gal who hasn't found a job yet."

"Who's the whiner?" I said.

"I'll never tell," he grinned. Then he went on to say that Jack Frazier's favorite juror would be a three-hundred-pound mother of eleven from Harlem—"Because they're all heart." Jurors with children were tops on the list in a case involving a baby. And blacks were better than whites, because they understood persecution. In fact, Jack Frazier always looked for people who'd had hardship in their lives: They could better understand the hardship in other people's lives. "Jack Frazier won't take Jewish women," Hannes Leeser said. "Too many doctors in the family. Especially unmarried Jewish career women— they're too mean." He laughed.

"That's not funny," I told him. "It's racist and anti-Semitic."

"Look," he said, "when choosing a jury, a trial lawyer has to make decisions fast. He's got to stereotype! If Jack Frazier sees a guy with Gucci loafers and a Rolex watch, then he's already got *his*, and he'll have no empathy for the underdog. Yuppies just want to be entertained, like it's all some episode of *L.A. Law*. And thumbs down to anybody with a weak chin—Jack Frazier says every juror with a weak chin has given him trouble, without fail."

I wondered how Jack Frazier saw me and Loretta, if it was his job to sum up people so thoroughly on the spot.

For lunch Loretta and I ate in a coffee shop I picked out because it was called Ellen's. The owner was a former Miss Subways—a kind of mail-in beauty contest that was popular in the fifties and sixties. Back then, Loretta told me, four women competed for the title every month, their pictures splashed all over the subways. And now the winners of this long-ago contest covered the walls of this coffee shop—women with softly swirling hair and descriptions such as: "Peggy, petite and Brooklyn-born, plans to marry her childhood sweetheart . . . Patricia bowls a neat 200, crochets her own hats, and her steady is an ex-Navy man."

But the food was terrific. At least it looked terrific—Loretta had a cheddar cheeseburger. All I had was some crispy lettuce and sesame melba toast.

"El, you're looking thin," Loretta said. "Now I know you're not the type to go on a diet. So why aren't you eating?"

But I didn't know how to explain it. "Must be the trial," was all I said. "It's so exciting."

Loretta bulged her eyes at me. "A three-hour wait is exciting?"

six

It began—suddenly.

"Hear ye! Hear ye!" Hannes Leeser called out, just moments after Loretta and I got back from lunch and planted ourselves on our bench. "All persons having business in this part before the Honorable Madam Justice come forth and be heard. Case on trial: Gray versus Niles."

And then eight people slowly, hesitantly came into the room through an oak door to the judge's left. A bit awkwardly they filed into the jury seats, as if only rehearsing this entrance. Jack Frazier sat calmly at a long oak table just in front of us; Charles Friss, from his long oak table on the other side, stood soldier-style erect, and didn't sit down until the last juror had taken his seat. A painfully thin man, almost gaunt, with fluttery, half-closed eyes, sat in front of the judge with what looked like a tiny typewriter on a tripod.

The jurors glanced at us, and glanced away. Which one was the whiner? It could be a contest, like finding Waldo. Raise your hands, those of you with hardship in your lives!

I whispered to Loretta, "Mom, there are eight jurors, not twelve."

Jack Frazier's back twitched slightly.

"Good afternoon, ladies and gentlemen," Judge Patterson began, in a deep, warm, clear voice, and the thin man's fingers came to life on the tiny typewriter—pressing down fleetingly, then rearranging his fingers lightning fast, and pressing down again. It looked like silent piano playing. Loretta had told me that court reporters take down in shorthand every single word of the trial. "My name is Evelynne Patterson, and I wish to apologize for the long delay. Mr. Leeser told me you were all patient and understanding, and I wish to thank you." She spoke with genuine respect.

Judge Patterson told the jury that first, both attorneys give opening statements. Then Jack Frazier brings in all of his witnesses, and then Charles Friss brings in his. After a witness testifies, the other lawyer can cross-examine that witness, and the first lawyer can ask some more questions. Like a tennis match, I thought, back and forth, with the witness as the ball. Then Jack Frazier and Charles Friss give their closing statements, and finally the jury goes off to consider its verdict.

"You bring to this courtroom all the experience and background of your life," Judge Patterson told the jury.

It was different, for me. This *was* the experience and background of my life.

"Your knowledge will help you determine who is

reliable, who is lying, and who is telling the truth."

What! The judge said right out loud that somebody was going to lie! But wasn't that illegal? Wasn't that doubly illegal, to commit a crime in a court of law?

But none of the jurors seemed surprised. One woman, I noticed, looked quite a bit like Loretta. And there was an older black man with spiky gray hair, and a redheaded woman, and a Latina woman, and an older black woman, and an Asian man, and a young black man, and a young blond woman in braids. Black, white, young, old—I was seeing only their surfaces. And these eight strangers saw only the surfaces of me and Loretta. The surfaces of fractions—that must be the tiniest of particles.

Judge Patterson said, "Do not discuss this case. Do not speak to the lawyers or witnesses. Do not consider them rude when they do not speak to you. We call this a 'ban on contact,' and it's in full effect until the trial is over. Now let's take a short break before the openings."

Charles Friss stood stiffly as the jury left. Jack Frazier's arm was draped over the back of his chair. But the moment the jury was gone, Jack Frazier leaped up and pointed accusingly at Charles Friss.

"I don't want him bowing and scraping for the jury!" Jack Frazier shouted, his face darkening. "He rises, I remain seated—how does it look?"

I actually shuddered. Jack Frazier had some temper! I never wanted to be on the other side of it. That seemed worse than sitting on the other side of the room.

"I'm not feeling so hot," Charles Friss said in a thin, high-pitched voice. "And he's yelling already."

"Mr. Frazier," Judge Patterson said with emphasis. "Please don't raise your voice. Mr. Friss is free to stand—"

"It's pretentious!" Jack Frazier yelled, the back of his neck turning rash red. "He's hopping up and down as if they're royalty, and I'm down here—come on!"

"I'll stop, Your Honor," Charles Friss said mildly, "if it will please Jack."

"It pleases me," Jack Frazier snapped.

Judge Patterson sighed, as if she were a fifth-grade teacher and these were her most naughty boys. It bothered me, hearing Charles Friss say "Jack." I knew Jack Frazier would never be friends with Charles Friss, the enemy.

Jack Frazier glanced back at me. As he approached me, there was an edge in his voice: "I heard you whispering. No talking, remember?"

"There were eight of them," I answered in a small voice. "Not twelve."

Jack Frazier exhaled deeply. His breath smelled of cinnamon gum, but he wasn't chewing. "In a civil trial," he explained evenly, "there are six jurors, and two alternates in case any of the six become ill or otherwise unavailable. A question like that can wait, can it not?"

I nodded.

"I want to hear nothing from you. I want to see only a calm, attentive young woman, like that well-behaved young man in the back."

Sam! I clenched my teeth. "Yes, Jack," I said icily.

Jack Frazier seemed a bit taken aback, and he frowned. There was that click again—something was shifting inside Jack Frazier. "Elena," he said softly, and paused. I waited for more. *Talk to me*, I almost said. But it was as if he was telling me, *You and I, we can talk without words.*

"We are traveling companions," Jack Frazier began his

opening statement to the jury, in a rather loud voice. "We are going on a long journey, and our destination is the truth."

Besides me, Loretta, and Sam, there was only Judge Patterson, the jury, Charles Friss, Hannes Leeser and Sheila, and the court reporter with the fluttery eyes. What had I expected—a roomful of curious spectators, and reporters, even? I'd thought the trial would feel so out in the open. It surprised me that it could feel private, enclosed.

Jack Frazier held out his arms as if gathering all the jurors into a bouquet. I felt a little swept up too. "Go back," he said, "go back to a night four and a half years ago. Loretta Gray," he gestured to my mother, "was pregnant. A beautiful, low-risk pregnancy with no problems at all. Loretta Gray found herself going into labor, two and a half weeks before her due date." His voice grew much louder and his accent heavier. He filled the entire room, even its cracks, like insulating foam. I felt as if my blood were moving faster through my veins, and my cheeks grew warm. The redheaded juror—first row, center seat—stiffened. I hardly blamed her. That kind of intensity could be frightening. And Jack Frazier was right on top of her!

"Loretta Gray's husband was away. Her first child, Ellen, twelve at the time, and who you see before you today at sixteen . . ." For a moment all eyes were on me, so quickly I didn't have time to get self-conscious about it, like people in TV audiences who calmly see themselves up on a monitor and then react just as the camera pulls away. "Ellen was at a slumber party. Ladies and gentlemen, Loretta Gray was utterly alone. But she called the hospital.

She phoned a relative to take care of Ellen. In the throes of painful labor"—and here he clasped his hands to his own abdomen, and I felt a tug on my own body—"she walked down three flights of stairs and got herself into a taxi. She acted carefully and responsibly, but was she treated that way at Sussex Square Hospital? No! She received shoddy treatment! Shoddy!"

"Objection!" Charles Friss called out. "We're not talking about Sussex Square Hospital! We're only talking about Dr. Warren Niles and—"

"He can only object!" Jack Frazier said to the judge. "He can't make speeches!"

"Objection sustained," Judge Patterson said. Loretta had told me that "sustained" means the objection stands, and the statement or question has to be withdrawn or rephrased. "Overruled" means the objection is rejected. "Mr. Friss, when you object, just say 'objection,' nothing more. Mr. Frazier, do not discuss hospital staff or procedure. Members of the jury, the lawyers may bicker. Please don't pay attention to it."

Why couldn't Jack Frazier discuss hospital staff or procedure? I'd thought that during the trial all the facts would come spilling out like sheets of rain from dark clouds. The young Latina juror, whose hair was swept back in a crimson headband, gazed ahead intently. The Asian man was frowning.

"Mrs. Gray learned some distressing news when she arrived at Sussex Square Hospital," Jack Frazier went on. "Her obstetrician, Dr. Paul Walker, had had a stroke. Sadly, Dr. Walker died a year ago, after suffering a second stroke. Tragedy for Dr. Walker, tragedy for Loretta Gray, tragedy for her baby." Jack Frazier lowered his voice. For the jury, he was two different people—one calm and low-key, the other all charged up and racing—and without warning he changed from one into the other. Hannes Leeser watched him with admiration. Sheila read papers at her desk. "Dr. Warren Niles was called in as a replacement. How sad for Loretta Gray, how sad for her baby! For if Dr. Warren Niles had shown simple human concern instead of failing so miserably, Barry Gray would today be a normal child with every opportunity before him, and not the seriously impaired little boy you will have the opportunity to see."

Seriously impaired little boy? But Barry had mild cerebral palsy—*mild*.

Charles Friss yawned. I heard a woman's voice behind me call out, "Where's the ladies' room?" Sheila pointed her thumb upstairs.

"The public myth is that only very bad doctors commit malpractice," Jack Frazier said. "Ladies and gentlemen, does it help Loretta Gray to know that Dr. Niles has delivered hundreds, perhaps thousands, of healthy babies? Are we to say, 'Every dog is entitled to one bite'?"

"Objection!" Charles Friss said. "Comparing my client to a dog—give me a break!"

"Please, Mr. Frazier," Judge Patterson said. "Mr. Friss, please. To object is sufficient."

The woman who looked like Loretta listened calmly, unaffected by tempers flaring up. The young black guy—who was very good-looking, and whose khakis and white T-shirt looked straight out of a Gap window—seemed annoyed by it.

Jack Frazier clasped his hands. The sound shot through me, like a car backfiring. He said, "You will hear what happened to Loretta Gray at the hands of Dr. Warren Niles. You will understand that his mistreatment of her caused Barry Gray's injuries. And you will want to compensate Barry Gray." The young blonde in braids, wearing a yellow sundress, gazed ahead a bit distractedly. "You see Barry Gray's devoted mother. You see his sister, Ellen, who, at an age when most girls fall in and out of love every week, has her head on straight and is happy to spend time with her brother." And Jack Frazier spun around to give me a tiny wink.

That was when it happened. Now it was my turn for something to shift inside me. What I felt for Ray Frost—a puddle. This was the Mediterranean Sea.

"I am confident you will have enough evidence to come to a just and fair verdict for Barry Gray and his family," Jack Frazier said, finishing up.

Funny Jack Frazier should mention falling in and out of love. I had fallen in love with Jack Frazier.

seven

As soon as Judge Patterson called for a break, Jack Frazier got up to leave the courtroom. I stopped him at the swinging door. "Jack," I said breathlessly, but no words followed.

"Yes, Elena?" Friendly enough, but with an undercurrent, like there was a meter running out somewhere and he'd used up all his quarters.

"Good opening," I told him.

"Thank you."

This trial could bring us together, I was thinking. It could be like the background music to a movie, the action happening all around the real story. *Us*.

"Why—?" I wanted to say *Why are you* you?

"Why what?" His tone was one degree sharper.

"Why did you become a medical-malpractice lawyer?" Jack Frazier cleared his throat. "Because it's hard, challenging work. Because the money's good. Because I don't like to see the bastards get away with it." He paused. "Anything else?"

I nodded. I had to keep him here. "Are you a runner? I mean, you look like a runner."

"Yes," he replied. "I run marathons, in fact, when I'm not busy on trial—as I am right now. Anything else?"

Are you married? Are you in love? But I just shook my head. After Jack Frazier left, the door swung back and forth drunkenly.

Charles Friss popped two pills in his mouth and drank some water from a tiny paper cup before speaking. "Ladies and gentlemen," he began, in his high, thin voice, "I'm not feeling so hot. But don't worry, I'll be okay." He sounded casual and friendly, a guy you'd meet at a backyard barbecue. The enemy, I had to remind myself. The older black woman smiled to herself. "Let me tell you about Dr. Warren Niles," Charles Friss said. "He rushed to Loretta Gray's side in the middle of the night, even though she wasn't his patient. A helluva guy! But let me ask you this—have you ever met someone who was thoughtful, compassionate, dedicated, and competent, but didn't necessarily seem that way? Sure, you know the type. Dr. Niles plays his cards close to the vest, as they say. But make no mistake about it, he's a deeply caring individual."

This was Dr. Nile's own lawyer? The doctor must have ice in his veins.

"Jack Frazier made a strong statement to you. He cried 'medical malpractice!' in a crowded room. Well, I can make a strong statement too. As much as, or even more than, a dead baby, many women fear the birth of a handicapped child. This is the truth about Loretta Gray. She can't accept the fact that her child isn't perfect."

Loretta didn't flinch, but I let out a tiny gasp. Loretta had accepted Barry instantly, unbudgingly!

"Loretta Gray must blame *somebody* for her child's cerebral palsy. She can't blame herself, right? Can't blame God, right?" Charles Friss pointed at each juror, as if Loretta had considered the possibility that maybe one of them was to blame. "She's picked a most convenient victim—the doctor. Sure, why not sue the doctor? Everybody's doing it—it's the height of fashion!"

The man with spiky gray hair blinked, yawned, stretched.

"I'm very sorry Barry Gray has cerebral palsy." Charles Friss softened his voice. "You're probably sorry too. If you aren't, Jack Frazier will make you sorry. Me, I stopped crying when I was three years old, but Jack Frazier will tear your heart out. But there's no room for sympathy in this courtroom, and the judge will back me up on that. No sympathy!" Charles Friss coughed and pounded his chest. He drank some more water. Was he really sick, or was this his version of a wooden leg? After banishing sympathy from the courtroom, was he trying to get some for himself? The redhead looked concerned. I noticed that she had a weak chin. How had she slipped past Jack Frazier?

Charles Friss leaned his elbows on the rail in front of the jurors. "What's going on here? I'll tell you what's going on here. Modern medicine is so advanced, everybody thinks doctors can perform miracles. But sometimes a doctor does his very best and a child is born with cerebral palsy anyway. Ladies and gentlemen, that is the case."

And that ended our first day of the trial.

As soon as the jury left, Jack Frazier headed straight for me. "I heard that gasp," he said sternly. "Can't you control yourself?"

"It just—popped out," I stammered.

"I want you to be aware of everything you're not aware of!"

It sounded impossible. But I could do it. I could be perfect for Jack Frazier. "Jack," I said, "that redheaded juror—I don't think she's with us."

"Oh, her." He waved her away. "I was hoping she'd kick herself off, and I didn't want to waste a challenge on her."

"Challenge?"

"You're allowed a certain number of jury rejections. Some jurors reject themselves for you, saying they're too biased or whatever. Still, it doesn't matter. Even if she's Friss's juror, she's weak and won't sway anyone."

"Is she an unmarried Jewish career woman?"

Jack Frazier wrinkled his bushy eyebrows, casting shadows over his eyes. "She's married," he said. "Elena, I'll worry about the jurors. Don't you worry your pretty little head."

This was about as condescending as it got! But I was thrilled. Pretty—he thought I was pretty. It put me in such a good mood, I walked over to Sam and said casually, "So, what do you think of the trial so far?"

He mumbled something at me—it sounded like, "I'm worried."

"What?" I said. "I can't understand you."

That got him mad. "You don't understand me because you expect not to understand me! If you'd listen once in a while—"

"Forget it," I said, and walked away. Why did I bother with Sam, anyway? What could he possibly be worried about?

Outside, it was warm and sticky. I loved Jack Frazier. It had already become a fact about me, like brown hair and grayish eyes. Loretta wasn't ready to hear this yet, but I could talk to her about him all I liked, as long as it concerned the trial. "Mom, how come Jack Frazier couldn't ask about hospital staff or procedure?"

"Because we're not suing the hospital," Loretta said, "or anybody besides Dr. Niles."

"So he can't talk about, say, any of the nurses or anything?"

"That's right. It simply won't come up. You'll see, El, lots of things simply won't come up."

So, all of us sat together in that one big room, full of oak and light, but nobody was allowed to talk to anybody else ("ban on contact"), so nobody knew what anybody else was truly thinking or feeling, though everybody got looked at and scrutinized. And now Loretta was telling me that certain things could be talked about and other things couldn't, so that only a fraction of what actually happened could be brought out. We were all in this together, but altogether isolated, too, from each other and from the story itself.

Crossing Bleecker, Loretta and I passed a newsstand, and I stopped dead when I saw the headline in New York *Newsday*: I'LL BE YOUR SLAVE. Turned out a forty-four-year-old lawyer had fallen for a seventeen-year-old high-school girl. My heart pounded against my chest. Clearly the universe was telling me these things happen.

Loretta peered over my shoulder. "El, don't read that

trash. The man had to quit his job as an assistant district attorney because he propositioned a teenager. It's pathetic—and sad."

Forty-four minus seventeen was what, twenty-seven? There were twenty-nine years between me and Jack Frazier. As Loretta and I walked up the three flights of stairs to our loft, the echo of our footsteps filling the hall, I remembered something I'd once heard about Charlie Chaplin. Didn't he fall in love with a much younger woman? Didn't he actually marry her?

It was already another fact about me. I wanted to marry Jack Frazier.

The kitchen smelled of potato knishes from our bakery downstairs. It made my stomach grumble, but I ate only some prune whip yogurt. Loretta went to bed early, so I fed Barry macaroni and cheese with ketchup, his favorite dinner. Barry sat at the kitchen table in a low chair; this steadied his arms by raising them up, so his hands were free to move better. I sat sort of behind him, my arm around his thin shoulders and my hand on his thin wrist, guiding the spoon. It's a regular-sized spoon, with an easy-to-grip plastic handle; his dish is a kind of bowl-and-plate combination, with the bowl rising up on one side so Barry can catch his food without chasing it all over the plate. His cup looks like somebody took a bite out of the rim. That way he can drink without tilting his head way back.

"It was only a half day, more like a quarter day," I told Barry as he ate. "We sat around all morning, ho hum, and in the afternoon both lawyers got up and talked a little bit about the case."

"Questions," Barry said.

"That comes tomorrow," I said. "The first witness is Dr. Niles, the man who delivered you. Mom said he's what's called a hostile witness, because he doesn't want to talk to Jack Frazier."

After dinner we looked at Barry's favorite book, *Animalia*. It has huge, lush, colorful pictures of "a hidden land of beasts and birds"—different animals for every letter of the alphabet. I had to turn the pages because this book has regular paper pages, which Barry would rip. He can turn the pages only in books made of extra-thick cardboard.

One of our "games"—actually a form of therapy—is for Barry to trace pictures with his finger. On the *H* page, while Barry was moving his finger up, down, and around one of the Horrible Hairy Hogs Hurrying Homeward on Heavily Harnessed Horses, he stopped and pointed to an eagle about to land in a pale green meadow.

"Duck," he said.

"No, Barry, it's an eagle. See his beak? See his talons? Watch my mouth. Eagle."

"Duck!" Barry said with energy, blue eyes fixed on the page.

"Barry, let's try something else. Where's the eagle?" Barry didn't respond. "What's the eagle doing?" More silence. "He's flying down from the sky. What time of day is it? Well, it could be dawn or dusk, right?" Claire had told me to practice "wh" questions with Barry—where, what, when, who, and, also, how. "Barry, say 'dusk.'"

"Duck!" Barry insisted.

"Barry, I keep telling you, it's an eagle—" I stopped right there. Barry learned at exactly his own pace. "It's all right," I told him. "You're just confusing eagles and ducks. Besides, it's probably a hawk, for the *H* page."

Barry slapped the *H* page. "My walk funny. My talk funny."

I felt a kind of heaviness in my chest, a weight. The weight of Barry. But I had no right to feel that way. Barry was exactly who he was supposed to be. "Listen to Nellie," I said. "You can walk all by yourself now. Remember, you used to need a walker?"

"Diapers," Barry said, pulling at the diaper beneath his shorts–the extra-large diapers for big boys we had to order from a special catalogue.

"You'll get potty trained when you're ready," I said. "Barry, listen, you must be smart, or you wouldn't be having these thoughts about yourself. Understand?"

But Barry was lost in staring at the *H* page, at a pitchfork of lightning in a burnt-orange and black sky.

eight

"Do you swear to tell the truth, the whole truth, and nothing but the truth?" Hannes Leeser held out a Bible for Dr. Warren Niles in the witness box.

"I do," Dr. Niles replied, and sat down.

That first moment of Dr. Niles's testimony felt exactly like a TV show. Nothing that followed did.

I'd awakened that morning trying to imagine Dr. Niles, the enemy. But none of the faces that had flashed through my mind—dark and brooding, old and gnarled, handsome and cruel—fit the man I saw now. And the real Dr. Niles didn't feel right either. He sat almost motionless in the very back of the witness chair, as if he wasn't really there; his voice, as he spelled out his name and recited his address, was quiet, flat; he never looked at me or Loretta, and only occasionally glanced at Jack Frazier or the jury. Instead he stared at the court reporter, as if dictating a letter to a secretary. He wore a blue suit, white shirt, and blue tie; his clothes fit the grudging way he talked (after all, he had to wear *something*). He had short, clipped hair, brown turning gray, a wide face, gold-rimmed glasses (I couldn't see the color of his eyes), and skin whose color could only be called colorless. Dr. Niles had shown up, but that was about it.

Barry was right. Basically, testimony was questions, question after question after question. I guessed that a lot of them had to be asked, to set the stage for even more questions to come. Why else would Jack Frazier hammer away at Dr. Niles with such boring, stilted, obvious questions such as: You and I have not met before today, have we, Doctor? Are you a physician licensed to practice medicine in New York? Did you work at Sussex Square Hospital four and a half years ago? Were you a colleague of Dr. Paul Walker's? Were you called in to deliver the baby of Loretta Gray? It was as if you walked into a restaurant and the waiter demanded to know, "Do you intend to eat a meal here? Are you familiar with the word *menu*? After you order your food and eat your meal, do you intend to pay for it?"

Jack Frazier wore an olive-green suit that brought out the green in his eyes (I had no trouble seeing that, even at a distance). There was a new court reporter—a young woman with shocking blue eyeliner, a black beehive, and a low-cut sweater that displayed a cleavage Jack Frazier probably considered in contempt of court.

Loretta did a beautiful job of watching Dr. Niles and betraying no emotion, even as the details of that night came out, little by little. I got completely caught up in the story, almost as if it had nothing to do with Barry, my

Barry. And it was a kick watching Jack Frazier. His words dueled with Dr. Niles, but he looked only at the jury. And his eyes reacted to every answer he heard, sometimes with fury, sometimes with mocking scorn.

"When you met Loretta Gray in the early-morning hours of February 22, four and a half years ago, what did you know about her, Doctor?"

"She was thirty-five years old," Dr. Niles responded. "She'd had one healthy child previously. Her pregnancy had proceeded without complication." It sounded like a list: Drop off laundry. Pick up dinner. Walk dog.

Jack Frazier said, "Loretta Gray didn't smoke or drink, did she, Doctor?"

"As far as we know."

"Doctor, please! It's on her record!"

"Physicians do not observe their patients twenty-four hours a day."

Jack Frazier seemed one inch away from exploding. I wanted to calm him down—get him to breathe deeply, drink some herbal tea. Maybe I could learn massage?

"What was the baby's heart rate, Doctor, on admission?" Jack Frazier said "doctor" as though it were a harsh and dangerous title, like "embezzler."

"One hundred and fifty," Dr. Niles answered.

It sounded absurdly high, but more questions revealed that this was a totally normal heart rate for an unborn baby—between one hundred and twenty and one hundred and sixty. How interesting! The study of the human body—this was something Jack Frazier and I could share.

Several people entered the courtroom and exchanged a few quiet words with the judge. But the trial didn't screech to a stop, which surprised me. Absentmindedly I glanced behind me, at Sam. What a ferocious look he threw back: Turn around! Sit straight! Don't fidget!

"Doctor," Jack Frazier clipped off, "when you examined Loretta Gray, what did you find?"

"That she was in labor. She had contractions. But the baby's head was high and her water had not broken."

This was when the testimony got technical, but I followed it closely, carefully. For all of pregnancy, a baby floats around in a bag of waters in his mother's womb. In the last weeks of pregnancy, usually the baby, head down, moves into the mother's pelvis. This is called an "engaged head." (Dr. Niles and Jack Frazier talked about "engagement" so much, I was sure somebody was getting married.) Just before labor begins, the bag of waters breaks, releasing a gush of water. In Loretta's case, the baby's head wasn't in the pelvis, and the bag of waters didn't break when she went into labor.

"Why is this combination of circumstances dangerous, Doctor?" Jack Frazier asked.

"It is not necessarily dangerous," Dr. Niles said.

Jack Frazier stood frozen and his jaw dropped. "Not dangerous?" he said, aghast. "A situation crying out for a prolapsed cord—not dangerous? Don't you consider a prolapsed cord one of the most terrible, dire, life-or-death emergencies in all of medicine?"

"It is serious, yes," Dr. Niles conceded.

"Tell the jury!" Jack Frazier shouted. "Tell the jury what a prolapsed cord is."

I learned—and so did everybody else—that a prolapsed cord was something that could happen to the baby's umbilical cord. The umbilical cord is the baby's pipeline and lifeline to his mother, supplying the baby with oxygen and nourishment. Sometimes, during birth, the cord can get squeezed between the baby's head and the bony wall of the mother's pelvis. And the baby suffocates.

"Doctor, did you consider the possibility of a prolapsed cord when you first saw Loretta Gray?"

"It is always a consideration."

"And yet you did nothing?"

"I did what was appropriate under the circumstances."

Jack Frazier asked Dr. Niles exactly what was appropriate under the circumstances. Dr. Niles said he placed Loretta Gray under observation. For how long? Three hours. Why three? Jack Frazier wanted to know, why not one, or two, or nine? He sounded more and more disgusted, as if Dr. Niles's very presence was poisoning his system like toxic fumes. Dr. Niles said he wanted to see how Loretta Gray's labor would progress, and three hours seemed sufficient.

"What did you do during those three hours, Doctor?"

"I don't remember. It was four and a half years ago, sir."

"Was your memory better a year ago, during your EBT, when you told Mr. Friss you did paperwork in your office?"

"If that's what I said, then that's what I did."

"It was the middle of the night, Doctor. Did you go back to sleep?"

"No, sir."

"Do you have a couch in your office?"

"I did not sleep, sir." For once Dr. Niles was emphatic.

The older black woman smiled to herself. But maybe she had a habit of doing this.

"After the three hours, what did you do?"

"I examined Mrs. Gray again. Her labor was not progressing sufficiently. I decided to break the water myself."

"How did you break the water, Doctor?"

"I inserted a long, thin, hollow needle into the bag of waters."

I cringed a little. Another juror, the woman who wore colorful headbands, tightened her body into itself.

"And then what happened, Doctor?"

"The cord prolapsed."

"How do you know?"

"I could feel it."

I had a sudden image of Dr. Niles's colorless hands inside my mother, touching her so intimately, touching Barry. How would my father feel, hearing this? Sad, angry, full of pain, pushing the pain away?

They talked about the baby's heart rate. It had plunged to fifty. This low heart rate meant Barry was "in distress." Dr. Niles said that he ordered an emergency cesarean section. A C-section, as he explained, means cutting a woman's abdomen and lifting a baby out. But before Loretta could be sliced open, Barry was born naturally.

"How long was Barry Gray in distress, Doctor?"

"Eleven minutes."

I looked down at my hands. Eleven minutes of suffocation. I held my breath and counted slowly, silently. I barely made it to eleven seconds before I had to breathe again. How on earth did Barry survive?

"What color was Barry Gray at birth, Doctor?"

"Slightly blue," Dr. Niles said. "That is not unusual, even for normal babies."

"I am not asking about normal babies, Doctor! I am asking about little Barry Gray!" Jack Frazier was incensed, hands on hips, scolding. "Doctor, was Barry Gray breathing at one minute of life?"

"No, sir."

"Wouldn't you say that's a bad sign?"

"No, sir," Dr. Niles replied, unruffled. Loretta had said the trial was particularly stressful for the doctor. So why didn't Dr. Niles seem all that stressed out?

"Doctor, did you think Barry Gray might be brain damaged?"

"The baby's color grew pink," Dr. Niles said. "By five minutes of life his heart rate was back up to normal. No, I did not think the baby was brain damaged."

"Doctor, oxygen loss for longer than four minutes destroys brain cells! Barry Gray suffered oxygen loss for eleven minutes!"

"Many babies go through similar births and emerge unharmed—"

"I am not asking about other babies, Doctor! I am asking about little Barry Gray!"

"I don't know why Barry Gray is brain damaged, sir."

Jack Frazier spun around—in shock, horror, outrage, disbelief. "Are you actually telling this jury that Barry Gray suffocated for eleven minutes and you don't know why he's brain damaged?"

"Yes, sir," Dr. Niles said simply.

"Is it at all possible that the loss of oxygen—"

"No, sir," Dr. Niles cut him off.

"You mean, Doctor, that you don't know the cause of Barry Gray's brain damage, but you know what wasn't the cause?"

Charles Friss called out, "Hey, leave him alone, already!"

Judge Patterson agreed.

We broke for lunch, and as soon as the jury left, Jack Frazier turned to give me and Loretta a heart-stopping grin. He looked utterly pleased and happy. "It's so beautiful out," he said. "Why don't you have lunch in the park?" It sounded more like a command than a suggestion.

I said, "Why don't you join us?"

Jack Frazier sighed loudly. "I wish I could, Elena. But work I must." And he turned back to his table.

I couldn't resist leaning over the rail. "Jack," I said.

He reluctantly turned around.

"Barry suffered a loss of oxygen for eleven minutes," I said. "How did he survive—?"

"Partial loss," he cut me off. "Total loss? Nobody could survive that." There was a hint in his voice. This was a dumb question.

As I turned around, I caught sight of Sam. He looked pale, a bit shaken. I couldn't help going over to him and asking, "What's the matter with you?"

Sam blinked. "What's the matter with me?" he said, incredulous.

"Yeah," I said, already sorry I'd asked.

"What's the matter with you, Ellen? Or should I say *Elena*?"

That got me mad. I wanted to say something devastating, but when I opened my mouth, no words came out.

"Ellen, the testimony," Sam said, almost pleading. "Didn't you hear it? The guy takes a three-hour nap and then botches up a procedure and gives your brother brain damage! If I look a little upset, maybe that has a little something to do with it!"

Something inside me softened. Still, that crack about

Elena. "Thank you for your concern," I said as politely as I could.

Sam shook his head at me, that head full of gray hair.

There'd been a wedding in Thomas Paine Park—a tiny, egg-shaped park full of tall trees and lush grass just across from the courthouse. A series of long tables with white tablecloths held row after row of plastic champagne glasses. Loretta and I bought lunch from a vendor and sat on a bench. The bride and groom had left, but the reception was still going strong—women in sweeping silk dresses and men in pinstriped suits. Drinking, eating white cake, laughing. On the other side of the park, I spotted a juror, the one who looked like Loretta, eating a gyro beside the man with spiky gray hair.

"Mom, what do you think the jurors talk about, since they can't talk about the trial?"

"The trial, of course," Loretta answered, biting into tuna salad on a hard roll. "El, plain yogurt—again? Your face is getting so thin."

I didn't mention the safety pin I'd had to put in my skirt. "But they're not supposed to talk about the trial," I said.

"Jack says it's good when jurors show a slight rebelliousness, break the rules a little."

When did Loretta and Jack Frazier have conversations when I wasn't around? Several people toasted somebody and clinked glasses soundlessly.

"Sam was upset," I said. "Because of what Dr. Niles did to Barry."

Loretta nodded.

"Mom, are you sure, I mean absolutely sure, that Barry has cerebral palsy because of Dr. Niles? I mean, I'm no doctor, I don't understand everything a baby goes through in order to get born. How do we know it's really Dr. Niles's fault?"

"I had my doubts too," Loretta said. "When I first went to Jack Frazier's law firm, I said the exact same thing—was it really the doctor's fault? Because if it wasn't, I wanted no part of it, and it turns out neither did they. I was told that if Barry's case got accepted, it would be because an independent panel of two doctors and a lawyer said it was a good case. This panel is paid only to give an opinion. And they don't want to tell the firm to take on a case that's likely to lose—in fact, they reject nine cases out of ten. Jack Frazier doesn't seem like the type who likes to lose, right?"

I agreed.

"The panel was unanimous on Barry's case. That was good enough for me."

I looked at Loretta's clear, smooth skin, at her sun-drenched hair. Something had settled itself inside her. "Mom, isn't it hard for you, seeing Dr. Niles?"

Loretta shook her head. "I wondered if I'd feel plunged back in the past, like I was trapped in some kind of emotional time machine. But the trial is having the opposite effect. All I'm concentrating on is getting through this, getting on to our future." She smiled. She had beautiful teeth. "I'm lucky, too. Dr. Niles is an absolute stranger to me—I don't remember his face from that night."

nine

"Doctor, what is a double setup?"

I had no idea how Jack Frazier could do it, but his voice seemed to come from different parts of the room. I'd thought maybe a juror had called out this question.

"A double setup means to prepare a room for either a cesarean section or a natural delivery," Dr. Niles stated in his matter-of-fact way.

"How long does it take to set up a C-section, Doctor?"

"Forty-five minutes."

"In an emergency?"

"About fifteen minutes."

This afternoon there was yet another court reporter—a woman with short curly brown hair and large brown eyes. She tilted her head every so often, as if listening to music, trying to hear each individual instrument.

"Once a cesarean is set up, how long does it take to get a baby out? In an emergency, doctor."

"Fifteen minutes."

Jack Frazier did a wide-eyed double take. "Fifteen minutes? You know that's utterly absurd, don't you, Doctor? Did he tell you to say that?" Jack Frazier pointed at Charles Friss, who gave the jury a "Who, me?" look.

Dr. Niles said, "The answer to your question is fifteen minutes."

"Just so happens that fifteen minutes is a bit longer than the eleven minutes this baby was in trouble, isn't that right, Doctor? Fifteen minutes! How convenient! And how wrong! Would it surprise you if the most comprehensive textbooks state very clearly that cesarean sections can be done in less than four minutes?"

Dr. Niles let out a tiny cough, placing his fist near his mouth. Was he catching something from Charles Friss? "It would surprise me," he said.

Jack Frazier took several thick books off his table, and asked Dr. Niles if he "recognized these textbooks as authorities." Dr. Niles said no, and no again, and kept on saying no.

"Doctor, you're fully aware, I'm sure, from your many conversations with Mr. Friss, that if you don't recognize these books as authoritative, I can't quote from them?"

Dr. Niles didn't respond.

Jack Frazier shook his head with disgust. "All right, Doctor, tell me this." I noticed that the woman who looked like Loretta was gazing up at him, fascinated. Was she in love with him, too? "Did you have a plan, Doctor, in case the cord prolapsed when you broke the water?"

"I don't understand your use of the word *plan*."

"Doctor, when the head isn't engaged and the water hasn't broken, there's a twelve-percent chance of a cord prolapse. I'm asking you why you had no plan—"

"Twelve percent, no." Dr. Niles frowned.

"That statistic comes from one of the textbooks you won't let me quote. Twelve-percent chance. It's rather high."

"It's false."

"Doctor, Loretta Gray was waiting around for three hours. If you had set up a cesarean and had then broken the water, isn't it true that Barry Gray could have been delivered in less than four minutes, with no brain damage, instead of after eleven minutes?"

"I had no reason to set up a cesarean," Dr. Niles said.

That was when I felt it, tugging at me. *There's something wrong with Dr. Niles*. It was as though even the possibility of wrongdoing wouldn't—couldn't—enter his thoughts.

"Doctor, a little concern, a little foresight—"

"You cannot foresee a lightning bolt."

I remembered the lightning bolt on the *H* page, a pitchfork against a burnt sky.

"It wasn't a lightning bolt, Doctor. It was a reasonable risk—twelve percent, Doctor."

"That is a false statistic, Mr. Frazier."

This could go on and on, and I thought it might. But out of nowhere Jack Frazier snapped, "I have nothing more for this witness," and we broke for the day.

I got up and placed my hand on Jack Frazier's arm. It was like touching a piece of wood beneath his clothes. "Jack, I wanted to ask you about Dr. Niles," I whispered, even though Dr. Niles and Charles Friss were already out in the hall. "There's something about him, something unusual—"

"He's as typical as they come," Jack Frazier boomed back at me. "The guy who says 'It was all my fault' hasn't been born yet! Don't hold your breath waiting for this one to admit anything."

"No, that's just it, he'll never admit anything because he's—"

"Elena, must run!" he said, and run he did.

Loretta was talking and laughing with Sheila. When I tried talking to them about Dr. Niles, Sheila said, "Let me tell you something about doctors and lawyers. They're peas in a pod! Warren Niles has more in common with Jack Frazier than either one of them has to any of us."

I couldn't help it—I let out a gasp. But it was okay because the jury was out of the room. "Dr. Niles and Jack Frazier are nothing alike!" I breathed out.

"They're very much alike, my dear," Sheila said. "They both like control. They like it when people are submissive. Jack Frazier and Warren Niles would probably play racquetball together if they weren't opposing each other in court."

Clearly Sheila enjoyed telling me things like this. Sheila had four daughters. Maybe she treated them this same way. Then it occurred to me who to talk to, because who else would better understand one doctor than another?

"I suppose the easiest thing to say is that Dr. Niles is a cold fish and be done with it," Dr. Walter Spinak told me that night. "But it's more than that, isn't it?" We sat at a round wooden table in his living room sipping iced cinnamon tea, surrounded by Oriental rugs, museum posters of decades-old exhibitions, plush easy chairs, stacks of magazines, and cat hair. Outside, an ambulance wailed. Walter, Roz's father, was wearing a faded blue T-shirt and bleached jeans; he has frizzy eyebrows and a frizzy brown-and-gray beard. We'd had spaghetti smothered in garlic, and the smell of garlic was everywhere. "It sounds as though Dr. Niles must see himself as perfect and must appear perfect. Maybe he feels watched, judged. Of course now that he's on trial, that's exactly what's happening."

I leaned over to pet Smoky, Roz's skinny gray cat. Smoky lay on her side by my feet, breathing fast and heavy, as if she'd been running a race and not lying around all night. "But if it's so important for Dr. Niles to be perfect, why didn't he do the perfect thing? During the three hours, set up a C-section. It would've been so easy."

Walter shrugged. "Maybe Dr. Niles was distracted or exhausted," he said. "Ellen, you may never know for sure, because you'll never get to know him. There's something called a 'failure of will'—knowing the right thing to do and just not doing it."

"Have you ever been sued?" I asked Walter.

Walter laughed, a nervous laugh. "I don't want to jinx it by answering you directly," he said, and knocked the wooden table twice. "But the threat of a malpractice suit adds a layer of stress to an already stressful job. Doctors have to make life-or-death decisions, and you need a kind of distance to do this. But keeping up that distance is stressful in itself."

"Some doctors get too distanced," I said.

"Yeah," he said. "'Robo-docs.' It can begin in medical school. You're there to learn all about the body and spirit—the subject is wondrous! And the first thing you do is dissect a cadaver. So you joke about the dead guy. Later on, during the endless hours of intense study and the endless nights without sleep, you need to make more and more jokes. So you call a child born with multiple defects a 'garbageman.' A 'crispy critter'—that's a child who's been severely burned."

I put my hand to my mouth. "That's so awful," I said.

"Ellen," Walter told me firmly, "distance and all, most doctors care deeply about their patients and do the very best they can. They truly want to heal the sick."

I leaned back in my chair. "I know that," I said, a bit too quick.

Walter looked at me; I looked at Smoky. "When a doctor is falsely sued for malpractice, it's devastating. A dear friend of mine won his lawsuit, but said the experience left him feeling raped. The woman who sued him—literally he'd held her life in his hands, and he'd agonized over her treatment. Throughout his trial, he couldn't eat or sleep. He said it felt like grieving over the loss of a loved one. Now every patient looks like a possible suspect. He'll never get over it."

What about all the families, I wanted to say, who lost malpractice cases—eighty percent of all cases, according to Sheila. Wasn't that like rape too? Instead I said, "So what do you hear from Roz?"

Walter finished his tea. "Don't be anti-doctor," he said. "Don't close yourself off that way."

But I had to, to open myself up for Jack Frazier.

ten

Hannes Leeser greeted me the next morning with an enormous bran muffin wrapped in plastic. "You're not eating enough," he said, handing it over to me.

"Looks yummy," I said, shoving it in my bag. "I'll have it for lunch." Probably it had more calories than I'd eat in a week!

Now it was Charles Friss's turn to cross-examine the witness, Dr. Niles. Charles Friss, in a sky-blue suit and bright red tie, looked quite snappy. I'm not worried, everything about him said. There's been a misunderstanding. Let's clear it up!

"Doctor," Charles Friss said, with far more respect than Jack Frazier had, "the American College of Obstetricians and Gynecologists—do you consider them an authority?"

"Yes, sir," Dr. Niles said evenly, not responding to his own lawyer in any special or different way.

Charles Friss read from a textbook: "'Asphyxia'—that means loss of oxygen, folks—'around the time of labor and delivery can be a cause of cerebral palsy, but the asphyxia must be nearly lethal.' Doctor, did Barry Gray almost die?"

"No, sir."

Did he even come close to dying? Charles Friss asked him then. No, sir. Did he need life support? No, sir.

The sexy court reporter was back. In school you aren't allowed to wear skirts higher than four inches above the knee. She would have been sent home, but immediately!

"Doctor, did Barry Gray have seizures?"

"No, sir."

I felt Loretta stir slightly. I thought it was because she knew that in fact Barry did have seizures soon after birth, though no one had believed her at the time. But it was something else. Somebody was behind me. Not Sam, two rows back. Somebody close—breathing down my neck, you could say. I turned my head ever so slightly and caught a big whiff of Jean Naté. "Good morning, Ellen," Aunt Beryl whispered hotly into my ear. I didn't respond. Aunt Beryl tapped me on the shoulder, and I brushed her hand away as if it were a mosquito. Gently, I touched Loretta's arm. Gently, she touched me back. *I know*, her touch said.

"Ellen," Aunt Beryl whispered. "I'm here."

Jack Frazier didn't turn around, but Loretta and I knew he was fully aware of Aunt Beryl—and not happy about it.

Charles Friss was saying, "Barry Gray was fed through an IV—an intravenous tube. Does that mean he was brain damaged?"

"No," Dr. Niles said. "The infant had trouble eating. This is common."

I scanned the jury. Nobody paid Aunt Beryl any attention. In fact, the man with the spiky gray hair had fallen asleep!

"Doctor, in your twenty-seven years of treating thousands of patients, how often have you seen a prolapsed cord?"

"Rarely, sir. Only a couple of dozen times."

"So little? So you would say less than one percent of the time?"

"Yes, sir."

"How about twelve percent of the time, Doctor?"

"No, sir." Dr. Niles stared at the court reporter's black hair.

Then they talked about what a bad idea it would have been to prepare Loretta Gray for a cesarean section. The risk of a prolapsed cord was so slight; cesareans are expensive and the vast number of them are unnecessary; there was no emergency, therefore no need for an emergency cesarean.

Charles Friss opened his eyes wide. "But Doctor, when the cord prolapsed, you ordered an emergency cesarean right away!"

"Yes, sir. It might have taken her longer than eleven minutes to deliver naturally. In that case the cesarean would have been quicker."

Suddenly trumpets blared and drums pounded, the sounds penetrating even the closed windows. "I'm not competing with the Chinese funeral home!" Charles Friss said.

"It will pass," Judge Patterson said. I heard Aunt Beryl clear her throat, and the music died away.

"Doctor," said Charles Friss, "at any time in your vast

medical training and education, did you read, anywhere, in any textbook or medical journal, that when you have a high head and unbroken water, you must prepare a double setup?"

"No, sir," Dr. Niles said.

"That's all!" Charles Friss said happily, and we broke for lunch.

Immediately Jack Frazier demanded of Loretta, "What is she doing here?" His body temperature had gone up–I could feel it from several feet away. "Do you realize how this looks to the jury? As if the relatives are lining up for the money! They can't wait to split the millions!"

Loretta shot Aunt Beryl a harsh look. "I didn't know she was coming."

Aunt Beryl wore a pale peach silk dress with a peach pillbox hat. "There's a young man in the back," she said defiantly. "He's a spectator. Well, so am I–"

"He doesn't talk to the plaintiffs," Jack Frazier told her, so furiously he was spitting a little. "Don't you understand? It's not for me–it's for the baby!" It took me a moment to realize he meant Barry. "I don't want to see you here again," he said, and stormed out of the courtroom.

"What a horrible man," Aunt Beryl said.

"He's working very, very hard," I said. "He's under a tremendous strain."

"And I'm not?" Aunt Beryl removed her hat and adjusted her dark red curls.

Loretta said, "Really, Beryl, how could you just show up?"

"I'm part of this family too, aren't I? I offered to bring Anne and Mitchell." (Aunt Beryl, my mother's sister, had sort of adopted my father's parents as her own.) "They said Court TV was one thing, but they're too old for hours of sitting on hard benches."

Loretta shook her head slowly. My grandparents here as well?

"Anyway," Aunt Beryl said, "I brought a present for Barry." She rooted around in her purse and pulled out a T-shirt that said, IF YOU THINK I'M CUTE, YOU SHOULD SEE MY AUNT.

"I give up," Loretta said, turning to go. "Ellen, I'll see you out in the hall."

Aunt Beryl cupped the T-shirt into a little ball and stuffed it back in her purse. "Perhaps it's too small," she said.

"It's too—something," I said.

"Your Jack Frazier didn't mean it, what he said about the baby," Aunt Beryl told me. "He's only doing this for the money. You don't think he really cares about our family, do you?"

"I do," I said, with feeling.

"Wise up, Ellen. Whatever you win, your Jack Frazier gets one third. If it's a million, he gets three hundred and thirty three thousand dollars. Not bad for a few weeks' work!"

I was so tired of people telling me to wise up. Life had already wised me up. I was the sister of a handicapped child. I even dressed the part! "If we win," I said, "Jack Frazier deserves every penny. If it weren't for him, we wouldn't even have the money."

Aunt Beryl smirked. "You're so quick to defend him," she said. "Could it be we see Jack Frazier as a knight on a white horse, come to rescue the damsel in distress?"

I could feel my own body temperature rise. "I am not a

damsel in distress," I said evenly. "I do not need rescuing."

Aunt Beryl took a step back and looked me up and down. "Ellen you're gaunt!" she declared. "You're not on some foolish diet, are you?"

Aunt Beryl should talk. Last year for two weeks straight all she ate was cabbage soup—for breakfast, even.

I pulled the muffin out of my bag. "Wrong again," I said, tearing off the plastic and taking a big bite. It was dry and soft and had raisins in it.

Aunt Beryl readjusted her curls and asked me where the ladies' room was.

"Maybe I should take you," I said. "It's kind of awful—"

"I think I'm capable of going to the bathroom by myself, Ellen."

I invited her along, but Aunt Beryl did not join us for lunch at Ellen's. All I had was chicken broth (because of the bite of muffin). I sat beneath Marie, the Miss Subways who "works as a book clerk . . . lucky break for an ardent reader." Marie had a dreamy smile, dreamy eyes. She looked as if the photographer had instructed her, "You're thinking of your knight on a white horse, coming to rescue you."

There was an impatient eagerness about Jack Frazier, as if all the thoughts and questions inside his head were like children in a classroom: Call on me! No, me! "Doctor," he began his redirect examination, his voice at top volume already, "you've only seen prolapsed cords a couple dozen times in your career, only about one percent of the time. But how many of those women were like Loretta Gray, Doctor? How many had a high head and unbroken water?"

Dr. Niles was as steady as ever, observing the court

reporter cross and uncross her legs. "I do not have numbers in my head," he said. "Proportionately, it is the same. One percent of the time."

My stomach growled; I felt so sleepy. I needed more discipline! Jack Frazier said that on trial he slept three, maybe four hours a night, and ate only one meal a day.

"Doctor, you said oxygen deprivation had to be extreme to cause brain damage. Eleven minutes—don't you consider that extreme?"

"The oxygen loss did not cause the cerebral palsy. Many babies suffer oxygen loss for even longer and suffer no ill effects."

I expected Jack Frazier to yell, *I am not talking about many babies, Doctor! I am talking about little Barry Gray!* Instead he softened his voice and said, "Doctor, think of the drunk driver. He can drive around all night and cause no injury, correct? And on his way home he knocks down three pedestrians. Is it any consolation to the three victims that the drunk driver didn't harm countless others?"

Charles Friss jumped to his feet. "Your honor!" he called out. "First a dog, now a drunk driver—come on, lay off!" And he proceeded to have a hacking coughing fit, followed by pills and water.

At the end of the day, Sam came over to me. I noticed his gray hair looked fuller, as if he'd washed it and applied gel. "You look tired," Sam told me. "Go to bed early—you're testifying tomorrow."

How did he know? Was he keeping a scorecard of witnesses? "I can't go to bed too early," I said, and couldn't help sounding thrilled. "Jack Frazier is coming over tonight!"

Sam sort of frowned. "For dinner?"

"Oh, no! He's much too busy for that. He'll come

around eight, to help us with our testimony. My mother testifies first thing tomorrow morning, then Claire, then me." Sam was nodding; he already knew that. I'll change when I get home, I was thinking. Tank top, the red one, and my black jeans. I took a small compact out of my bag and looked in the tiny mirror, touching the dark circles beneath my eyes. I'd have to apply dark-circle concealer—probably with a spackle knife.

"I told you you looked tired," Sam said.

I snapped the compact shut. "At least I didn't fall asleep like one of the jurors!"

Sam grinned. "I noticed. Anyway, Hannes Leeser said sleepers are good."

I had to laugh. "Sleepers are good?"

"They already know what's going on, so they don't have to listen all the way through."

I shook my head. "I don't understand."

Sam looked at me intently, not blinking. "Inside each juror's head, there's a quiet little voice," he said. "Sometime during the trial, that voice whispers, 'Oh, that's it.' And the juror knows, he just knows. It can happen early on, during the *voir dire*, even, or later on, in deliberations." Sam was standing close to me. I could feel his breathing.

"A quiet little voice?" I said.

"A quiet little voice," he said back softly.

Loretta and I sat in easy chairs on either side of Jack Frazier, who sat on the couch with Barry in his pajamas. The rich, spicy smell of apple turnovers from the bakery downstairs breezed in through our open windows. Sometimes the bakery stayed open late like this, especially on beautiful summer nights.

"We're not rehearsing the testimony," Jack Frazier said. He'd taken off his jacket but kept his oxford-cloth shirt buttoned at the cuffs and neck. "Loretta, you can leaf through your EBT tonight, but don't memorize anything. You must appear spontaneous. The most important testimony is what's called 'demeanor testimony'—that the person you are shines through."

If that's true, will the whole courtroom know I'm in love with Jack Frazier?

"My questions will not be difficult," Jack Frazier said. "Loretta, I'll ask you what you remember about Barry's birth and infancy. Elena, I'll ask you about day-to-day life with Barry. On the witness stand, listen to me carefully. Keep your answers short. Speak loudly, clearly. Ever been in a play? Project." Absentmindedly, Jack Frazier stroked Barry's hair. Barry, who never let anybody touch his hair like that, was looking up at him, rapt. "Loretta, when Friss cross-examines you, no matter how belittling or sarcastic he is, don't lose your cool. It's what he wants, for you to appear unstable. Don't stop to figure out if your answers will help you or hurt you. You are sworn to tell the truth. Just tell it." Jack Frazier smiled his most charming smile. "I've always said that nine out of ten of my clients make my job tougher. I'm confident that both of you will be among those one-in-ten."

"One, ten," Barry said. "No—one, two."

Jack Frazier let out a big laugh.

"What should we wear?" I asked, eager to get Jack Frazier in my room to inspect my clothes. I had no overhead light in there, only two lamps, so the light was always cool and dim.

"You've both been dressing perfectly," he said. "Keep it up."

I sank back in my chair. Outside, brakes screeched on the cobblestone street.

Jack Frazier asked Loretta a few sample questions—to establish the right tone, he explained. Afterward he said, "Wonderful. But always be aware of yourself, especially when Chuck attacks you."

Chuck? "I'll beware—I mean, be aware, too," I said, "when Charles Friss attacks me." I emphasized *Charles Friss*, not Chuck. Surely Jack Frazier had made a mistake.

"Charles Friss won't attack you," he said. "You look older than sixteen, but the jury knows you're just a teenager, and Friss knows that cross-examining a child is a mine field. Friss will be gentle and delightful to you—and brief. For hours he will be a monster to your mother."

But maybe Jack Frazier was wrong about that, too. I doubted Charles Friss even had it in him to be gentle and delightful.

"I had a nine-year-old on the stand who was brilliant," Jack Frazier said. "Her mother died, a wrongful-death case. In court, I asked her, 'Who takes care of you now?' I expected her to say, 'My aunt.' Instead she answered, in a tiny, little voice, 'Me. I take care of me now.' The jury wept." He paused, remembering her.

I cleared my throat. "So, how is the little girl now?"

"Why, she must be twenty, a grown woman," Jack Frazier said, sounding a little surprised that little girls actually turned into women. "I have absolutely no idea."

I couldn't bear for that to happen. For the trial to end and for years to pass, with me ending up just a particle in Jack Frazier's memory.

eleven

The air conditioner broke that morning and the courtroom felt like a poached egg. Judge Patterson asked the jury if they could stand it, and everyone said yes except for the chinless redhead, who asked for a bowl of ice water and a washcloth for her forehead!

Loretta wore a silk dress, dark blue, and her just-washed, shining hair fell to her shoulders. Her skin looked radiant. I'd washed my hair, too, but didn't look all that radiant. My stomach growled so much, it kept me up half the night.

One hand on the Bible, Loretta swore to Hannes Leeser that she would tell the truth, the whole truth, and nothing but the truth. Then she spelled out her name, letter by letter, and slowly recited her address, as the sexy court reporter, forehead dripping with sweat, took it all down.

"Good morning, madam," Jack Frazier said politely,

looking directly at her. With Loretta on the stand, his gaze swept back and forth between the witness and the jury. He'd gotten a haircut that morning—the tight frizzy curls clung even closer to his head. "It's a bit warm in here. Are you uncomfortable?"

"I like the heat," Loretta said in a clear, strong voice—and, with that simple statement, set the tone for almost all of her testimony.

"Madam, are you the plaintiff in this lawsuit, on behalf of your son, Barry Gray?"

"Yes," Loretta answered, glancing at the empty benches, row after row, on the defense side. Dr. Niles wasn't there.

"You have another child, madam?"

"My sixteen-year-old daughter, Ellen," Loretta said, glancing this time at me.

"Is she a healthy child, madam?"

Loretta said yes. I wished I could be referred to as something other than "child"—and his calling her "madam" made her sound like the president's mother!

"Was your pregnancy normal?"

Loretta smiled slightly. "Dr. Walker said it was so normal it was boring."

Jack Frazier had instructed us, *Just answer the question!* But Loretta knew what she was doing.

When Jack Frazier asked Loretta what she remembered about that night four and a half years ago, the blonde in braids leaned forward, elbows on her knees.

"I was home," Loretta said, and Charles Friss began scribbling notes at his table. "It was late, midnight. My body felt tight, too tight, as if I had on clothing two sizes too small. The baby wasn't due for a couple more weeks, and my water didn't break, but I became concerned. I took a cab over to Sussex Square Hospital. I got undressed, put on a hospital gown, and got hooked up to a fetal monitor. I asked for Dr. Walker, and that's when I found out he'd had a stroke, and that Dr. Niles was replacing him. I said I didn't know any Dr. Niles, and a nurse told me, that's because he's new here."

"Do you remember the baby's heart rate?" Jack Frazier asked.

"No, but it was a three-digit number, over one hundred."

"Did anyone seem alarmed by what was on the monitor, or by what was happening to you?"

"No, sir. I was having contractions by then, but it was all business as usual."

"Madam, when did you meet Dr. Niles?"

"I guess about an hour later. As he examined me, I asked him, is Dr. Walker all right? He didn't answer. He told a nurse that he'd be in his office, and I didn't see him again for three hours."

"And what took place during those three hours?"

"Not much." Loretta paused. "Between contractions, I chatted with the nurses. During the contractions—well, there's not much you can do." Several jurors smiled. "I signed some insurance forms, had my blood pressure checked, things like that. When Dr. Niles got back, he looked me over again, and said, 'Let's break the water already. She's had one kid—she can have another.'"

Jack Frazier paused, looking at the jury long and hard. "Those were his exact words?"

"Yes," Loretta said. "Dr. Niles took out a needle. He told me to bear down. I didn't feel a thing. I remembered thinking how, with Ellen, there was a huge gush when the water broke. But I felt nothing. Suddenly Dr. Niles's mood changed, utterly. Before, he was calm. Now he was quite agitated."

"Objection," Charles Friss interrupted his writing to say. "Agitated—that's her opinion. He leaped into action, is more accurate."

But Judge Patterson said Loretta could describe what she remembered.

"Dr. Niles told a nurse to lean the bed back, so I was practically upside down—I remember my toes in the air, against the glare of the overhead light. Dr. Niles got on the bed with me. He put his hand on the baby." The chinless redhead dabbed her upper lip. "On the monitor—I don't remember the exact number, only now instead of three digits there were only two." Loretta shifted around in her chair. "I got so scared. Is something wrong? I kept asking; but nobody answered me. A nurse placed an oxygen mask over my face. I pushed off the mask and asked again, is something wrong? Now Dr. Niles was furious. He yelled at a nurse to set up a cesarean section. Dr. Niles, still on the bed with me, still with his hand inside me, kept yelling, hurry it up, hurry it up, as a nurse painted my stomach with a yellowish-brown solution. Dr. Niles yelled at me, too. I had to get that baby out, he said, push, push! But it was like pushing against cement. Dr. Niles kept yelling—is it set up yet? Push, push! And then Barry was born."

The courtroom was still, quiet. Jack Frazier let the moment linger, and then asked, "What happened next?"

"I waited for the baby to cry," Loretta said. "But he only squeaked, like a mouse. Before they took him away, I caught a glimpse of him. He was so still. And blue. It took my breath away." Loretta placed her fingers to her throat, as if holding the breath she had lost. "I was in a recovery room when they brought the baby back to me. His color was better, but over the next hour he turned blue four or five times."

"Did you mention this to Dr. Niles?" Jack Frazier asked.

"I never saw Dr. Niles again—not until two days ago."

Loretta went on to describe the Barry I remembered. How he wouldn't breastfeed, how he wouldn't even try to eat. How you had to tilt his head way back and let formula trickle down his throat. Even so, he spit up so much that meals took up to two hours—every day, day after day. How Barry barely moved at all, so you kept thinking he was asleep, but then you'd see his eyes wide open, staring. How his eyes sometimes flicked back and forth, from left to right, very fast—how those were tiny seizures. How he never cried.

"At six months," Loretta said, "Barry wasn't sitting up—he wasn't even trying to. I saw eleven doctors before I found one who diagnosed Barry with ataxic cerebral palsy."

"Madam," Jack Frazier said, "Mr. Friss accused you of being the type of person who could not accept her imperfect child."

Loretta shrugged. "It was far worse, before the diagnosis," she said. "Knowing with every cell in my body that something was wrong with my child, and not knowing what to do about it. Once I had the diagnosis, I could wrap myself around it. I felt freed—free to meet the challenge, free to be excited about the tiniest progress, free to adjust myself to become the best person I could be for my child."

"Thank you," Jack Frazier said softly, with real tenderness.

There was a short break before Charles Friss got his chance at Loretta. I was the first to congratulate her on how beautifully she was doing, and Sam came right after. Sheila gave her a thumbs-up sign. Only Jack Frazier seemed subdued. When I asked him about it, he whispered to me, "Wait and see, Elena. It's not the doctor who's on trial. It's your mother."

Charles Friss, in a somber black suit and tie, began his cross-examination of Loretta in a great hurry, as if he didn't have a moment to waste: "Mrs. Gray, did you review your transcript?"

"My script?" Loretta said.

"Your transcript, Mrs. Gray, your transcript! Did you review your transcript?"

"I—yes, I reviewed my transcript." Loretta sat with her knees together and hands folded.

"Mrs. Gray, are you a doctor?"

"I—what?"

"Are you a doctor, Mrs. Gray?" Charles Friss spoke loudly, carefully, as if she might have trouble understanding the simplest of concepts. "Shall I have Miss Drillings read the question back? Are you a doctor, Mrs. Gray?"

Poor Miss Drillings. She was sweating more than anybody, Loretta included.

Loretta responded, "I am not a doctor."

"You claimed in your EBT that Barry had seizures even in the hospital. You're a librarian, Mrs. Gray. In your spare time are you a doctor who can diagnose such things?"

"I know what I saw." Loretta was firm, calm. "When I

described Barry's behavior to the right doctor, I was told Barry was having seizures."

"Hey, the baby was flicking his eyes!" Charles Friss said. "Newborns are chockful of little tics and tremors. Hell, my son's eyes used to roll up in his head! How do we know you weren't exaggerating, so that in your fanatical pursuit, seeking out one doctor after another—and wasn't it twelve in all, Mrs. Gray?—you could get one to diagnose seizures!"

Loretta was frowning. "I didn't have to exaggerate."

Charles Friss grinned at the jury. "It was four and a half years ago, Mrs. Gray. You remember exactly what Barry's eyes were doing?"

"I remember like it was happening right here in this courtroom."

I could almost feel Jack Frazier relax, see his body loosen up. Loretta was a one-in-ten.

"Mrs. Gray, you claimed that Barry was blue. Really?" Charles Friss sounded incredulous. "Babies come out covered with blood, and you were terribly frightened—"

"I wasn't frightened. He was blue."

Charles Friss lunged a finger at her. "You testified that you were terrified!"

"Not by the sight of my baby," Loretta said.

I felt my throat close in on itself. My mother was under attack! I wished my father were here, with his calm, solid presence. I wished I could touch his arm gently, and he could touch my arm back: *I know.*

Charles Friss was saying, "A person who is frightened one moment can surely be frightened the next?"

"Mr. Friss, I am telling you how I experienced it."

Charles Friss laughed. "Exactly, Mrs. Gray, exactly!

How you experienced it. Which may or may not be how it actually happened. For instance, did it really take two hours to feed Barry, or did it only feel that way?"

"It took two hours," Loretta said.

"You had your eye on the clock, not on the baby?"

Charles Friss did not tire easily. It was sauna hot, yet he hammered away at Loretta: Had Dr. Niles really said, "Let's break the water already"? Four and a half years later, she remembered the precise words? Wasn't it possible that Dr. Niles chose not to converse with her about Dr. Walker because his mind was on far more important things—like her baby? While in excruciating pain, was she really reading numbers on a monitor—and upside down, at that! Was she lying, or bent on revenge, or just plain misguided? Or all of the above and more besides?

"Mrs. Gray," Charles Friss said, "I have no more questions."

Loretta looked so pleased that several jurors laughed.

Jack Frazier got up on his feet in an instant. "Madam, you are not a doctor, and many doctors said you were wrong about Barry. But, in fact, Barry Gray does have cerebral palsy. You were right all along, weren't you?"

"Yes," Loretta said.

Once the jury left, he put his arms around Loretta—or, rather, Loretta fell into them. "Not a trip to Disneyland, is it?" he said.

"No." She laughed. "I sure won't be sending out any picture postcards."

I asked Sam to join us for lunch, and he seemed genuinely disappointed that he had to spend the time running errands for Maribeth. Tomorrow, then, we agreed.

"It felt like a performance," Loretta told me at Ellen's,

on her second cheeseburger. "Loretta Gray playing Loretta Gray. I could almost see the list of characters in the *Playbill*—my name twice, separated by a line of dots. I felt so aware of myself, so aware of all those other eyes on me. The adrenaline—wow." She smiled. "I hope I'm not making you nervous, El."

"I'm not nervous, Mom." I was counting on all those eyes on me—especially Jack Frazier's, watching me stand up to Charles Friss, Joan of Arc style. I had a few bites of a clump of tuna fish sitting in a tomato half, cut to look like the bottom of a jack-o'-lantern's grin.

"It's funny," Loretta said. "Charles Friss made me so mad, and that actually felt good. Testifying is scary, especially those first few minutes—"

"You didn't look scared, not a bit," I said.

"Oh, but I felt it. And if my testimony had lasted only a few minutes, I might have stayed scared. But my own anger relaxed me. I even remembered what Roz said about the Wicked Witch of the West. Friss is the Wicked Witch, I told myself. All bluff and no power!"

twelve

The air conditioner was humming when we got back that afternoon, and the thin man had replaced Miss Drillings.

"Claire Withers Stonehill," Claire introduced herself to the courtroom. I've always loved her voice: careful and simple, like a machine that has never broken. A beige cotton suit was buttoned all the way up to her throat, and her skirt fell precisely below her knees. She always smells like clean, pressed laundry. She has huge brown eyes behind horn-rimmed glasses, and her gray hair, straight as thread, stops just above her ears. "I am Barry's therapist," Claire said. "I work with Barry every afternoon. In the mornings I work with a girl in Westchester."

This shocked me. I'd known Claire for two years, and until that moment had had no idea what she did with her mornings.

"Barry needs physical therapy because he cannot fully

control what his muscles do," Claire was saying. "My hands are trained to tell the difference, for instance, between Barry pushing his foot into my hand, or his leg involuntarily stiffening up. Barry also needs occupational therapy."

Jack Frazier circled in front of her. "Does that have to do with employment?"

"That is a common misunderstanding," Claire replied. "Occupational therapy helps the child achieve the greatest possible independence in daily life—washing, feeding, grooming, dressing. Barry requires speech therapy, too. I am helping Barry build up his 'inner language'—the language he hears inside himself. He knows a little Sign language, but the emphasis is on the spoken word. We read books together, slowly, intently, and talk about new words and concepts. We play together. Play is how children learn. We discuss important subjects. 'The dangers of strangers,' for example. Barry is far too trusting. Barry hugs people he doesn't even know."

Jack Frazier turned around. Again I could sense his relief. Claire was another member of the one-in-ten club. I was hoping to become its president.

Jack Frazier introduced into evidence Barry's IEPs—Individual Education Programs, yearly reports written by Barry's teachers at United Cerebral Palsy with some help from Loretta. They describe what Barry can do in September, what his goals for the school year are, how he will meet those goals, and his chances of "mainstreaming"—entering regular public school. "'Barry is shy and self-conscious,'" Jack Frazier read from the most recent one. "'Barry is passive.' Miss Stonehill, what's wrong with being passive?"

"It's an aggressive world out there," Claire said crisply. She talked about how, in the world of the handicapped, Barry was far from alone with this problem. Able-bodied kids were always shouting, "Now it's my turn!" and plowing ahead. "But you won't see handicapped children fighting over whose turn it is," Claire said. "They're used to waiting–they do it all the time. They are not spoiled." She cleared her throat. "Still, it's not good, not in today's world, when handicapped people must fight for what they need."

I thought about Sam. He was a fighter.

"What do you predict for Barry's future?" Jack Frazier asked, as if Claire Withers Stonehill had brought along her crystal ball.

"Barry has one more year at UCP. After that, I see him in MIS–Modified Instructional Service, ten kids to a class, or mainstreamed into what we now call 'inclusive classes.'"

The Asian man had fallen asleep, and the woman who looked like Loretta seemed in danger of nodding off. It worried me a little. I had to remind myself–sleepers are good.

"Would you say Barry is intelligent?" Jack Frazier said.

"I don't know his IQ," Claire said, bristling a little. She'd once told me she didn't trust IQ tests, that some of the smartest people she knew had absolutely average scores. "Barry wants to learn. To me, that's intelligent."

"Thank you," Jack Frazier said, and sat down.

There was no break. Charles Friss's first question was, "Miss Stonehill, are you getting paid for your testimony?"

"No," she said.

Charles Friss spun around. "You're kidding! Then

you're here because you work for Barry Gray's mother?"

"I am here because of Barry," she said, and blinked behind her glasses.

Charles Friss grunted as if he didn't believe her. "You're teaching Barry Gray about 'the dangers of strangers,'" he said. "But isn't this something that every four-year-old child should learn, handicapped or not?"

"Yes," Claire answered. "But Barry is particularly vulnerable—"

"Every four-year-old child needs to learn this, right?" Charles Friss cut her off. "Even among normal kids, some kids are more trusting than others, right?"

"Yes," Claire replied.

"Miss Stonehill, wouldn't you say Barry Gray has moods?"

"Moods? Yes, surely."

"And as he gets older, maybe he's getting moodier—I know I am!" Several jurors laughed. "Childhood is chockful of change and stress. Barry's shyness, his self-consciousness. Couldn't Barry be experiencing normal, little-boy moods?"

"I think it is more than that." Claire paused. "I may be mistaken."

"You may be mistaken about a lot of things, Miss Stonehill!"

"Move to strike!" Jack Frazier yelled.

"Yes." Judge Patterson glared at Charles Friss. "The jury will disregard that last remark."

Charles Friss smiled sheepishly at the jury, as if to say, I couldn't help it! "The same is true of Barry's passivity," he went on matter-of-factly. "Some children are simply more passive than others."

"In the world of the handicapped, Mr. Friss, in a world of passive children, Barry is particularly passive. Sometimes Barry grows lost in thought, to a place inside himself. I think as Barry grows older, he is becoming more aware of other children and of his own differences."

Charles Friss swatted the air. "Nothing else," he said.

Jack Frazier got up. "Miss Stonehill, are you giving your opinion to this jury as a casual bystander, or are you stating what you believe to be true based on years of training and experience and after spending hundreds of hours with Barry Gray?"

"Sir, I am answering as a professional."

And that was the end of Claire Withers Stonehill's testimony.

At the break I rushed up to Claire and told her, "You were great!"

"Adequate," Claire replied.

"Claire, I didn't know you worked with another child. Who is she? Is she like Barry?"

"Ellen, I do not discuss Barry with the other family. I will not discuss the other family with you."

That was Claire Withers Stonehill. Parts of her life did not spill over into each other.

I couldn't wait for this break to end. I was ready for my ten rounds with Charles Friss—more than ready!

But once the jury came back, Judge Patterson said, "I must attend to some business for the rest of the afternoon. My apologies to the next witness." And she sent everybody home—including me, the next witness! All this energy—what was I going to do with it?

"Sam," I stopped him at the door, "I'm all keyed up. Want to go dancing tonight?"

Sam looked at me, trying to see if I was serious. And his face darkened. "I—no," he said, harshly.

I watched him take off down the circular hall. Of course he didn't want to dance. He couldn't even walk without leaning over to the left. I wanted to say I was sorry. I could have caught up with him at the elevator. Instead I spent a few minutes with Jack Frazier, complimenting him on how well the day had gone.

I came home to a giant picture postcard from Ray of a covered bridge. *Dearest Ellen,* the card began. *I still need a title for my book. Could you put on your thinking cap—* I stopped reading. I'd never stopped reading a postcard before.

Loretta talked on the phone to Grandfather Mitchell, updating him on the trial, while I spent the evening with Barry. "Claire told everybody in the courtroom all about you," I told Barry. He liked that. We read some books, and I held Barry's hands as we danced to music (so much for Sam!), and after Barry's bath I put him to bed. He smelled like shampoo and pineapple. I kissed his forehead, soft as the smoothest velvet.

thirteen

"I call Ellen Gray to the stand," Jack Frazier said.

I got up and walked to the witness stand. There was a step up; I turned around. Suddenly I was so close to the jury! The chinless redhead wore heavy eyebrow pencil. The man with spiky gray hair had tiny dimples. I could see the shadows of the hollow cheeks of the thin court reporter, and Judge Patterson was practically sitting on my head. Across the room sat Loretta, who couldn't help smiling at me a little. The space beside her looked emptier than all the other empty benches. *Daddy's not here*, I thought. Two rows behind Loretta, there was Sam, utterly blank, no expression at all. Behind Sam was the clock: one minute after ten.

"Place your hand on the Bible," Hannes Leeser instructed me formally, as if we'd never even met. "Do you swear to tell the truth, the whole truth, and nothing but the truth?"

"Yes," I answered, and sat down.

"State your full name," Hannes Leeser said.

"Ellen Gray. E-L-L-E-N G-R-A-Y." I could feel my voice in my throat. *Where's Daddy?*

Jack Frazier got up. He looked . . . beautiful. Charcoal-gray suit that fit his body like the skin on an eggplant. I had on a sleeveless blue blouse and blue skirt, and had washed my hair again, so it got way too frizzy on this hot, humid day. I'd put on lipstick, but had rubbed it off. Cherries in the Snow, it was called. I'd bought it because of the name, but it was too red, too bright. Jack Frazier asked me his first question: "What grade are you in, Miss Gray?"

"Twelfth grade, sir. I mean, in the fall."

"But you're only sixteen. Isn't that a little young?"

"I skipped a grade," I said. *I'll be eighteen in a year and a half! Then we can elope!*

"And you consistently get good marks in school?"

"I try." Then I realized that Jack Frazier was showing off my intelligence, so I said, "I have a ninety-one average. This year I made the honor roll." I could almost feel Roz punching me in the arm—we are a bit full of ourselves, aren't we!

"Miss Gray, would you say you are involved in your brother's life?"

"Oh, yeah!" I said, and blushed a little. *Yes, sir* was the proper response. The juror who looked like a Gap poster smiled at me.

"Would you tell us what you do with Barry?"

"Yes, sir. We're always playing around and making stuff." Stuff—a kid's word. "Last month we made a poster called 'Barry's Red.' I helped him cut out pictures from magazines—he can't really use scissors by himself. We cut out a tomato, a bottle of ketchup, some lipstick, and a can of Hawaiian Punch. Then we drew red things on construction paper. Barry can't use regular coloring books—his hands press down too hard and he rips the paper. Barry has extra-thick crayons because thin ones break in his hands." This was going okay, like a well-designed car zipping down the open road. "Sometimes I place my hand over Barry's hand. Sometimes he likes to do it by himself."

"Thank you, Miss Gray," Jack Frazier said, and sat down.

What? *Thank you?* Was that all Jack Frazier wanted from me?

"Miss Gray." Charles Friss got up and smiled at me. To my horror, it was a genuine, friendly, honest-to-God smile. Was he the Wicked Witch—or Glinda? I got a bit dizzy. Suddenly I was feeling all those many meals I'd skipped, including that morning's breakfast.

"Miss Gray," Charles Friss said warmly, eagerly, "you're a helluva lot more perceptive, more mature, than other girls your age." Wait a minute. Charles Friss was saying nicer things about me than Jack Frazier had. "Wouldn't you say that having Barry for a brother has taught you many valuable things?"

This was a trick question. It had to be. "No," I said.

He let out a little laugh. "Of course you mean—"

"Yes," I snapped.

Several jurors frowned at me. No doubt about it, something was going horribly wrong. I glanced at the clock—10:02. But that couldn't be right! Was the clock broken again, or was time stuck? I felt warm all over—my body gathered heat, kept it close. Was I getting a fever?

"Miss Gray—"

I missed some words. Charles Friss smiled at me lovingly. Not you! I wanted to shout. You're all wrong, the altogether opposite person! My chest folded in on itself. "What?" I said. My lips stuck to my teeth. I wiped my mouth with the back of my hand. Blood. *Oh my God*.

"Miss Gray, I was asking how you felt about Barry—"

"I love him," I blurted out.

"Yes, of course," Charles Friss said encouragingly. "You've helped him so much—clearly you're a terrific person—"

My head felt swirly, like a dust ball. Help! my eyes pleaded to Jack Frazier. Get me out of this! But Jack Frazier was sitting back in his chair. In fact he was— yawning.

"Mmm-my-mmuh," I began to stutter. And couldn't turn it off. "Mmuhy—mmmuh—"

"Thank you, Miss Gray," Charles Friss said immediately. "You may step down."

But I just sat there.

"Let's take a fifteen-minute break," Judge Patterson said, and the jury left the room—more quickly than usual, I noticed.

The clock moved. Ten-oh-three. So, it was working after all. I'd only testified for two minutes. On my hand—not blood. Only Cherries in the Snow.

Loretta helped me down from the witness stand, and wrapped her arm around me. I couldn't feel it, only its weight. Jack Frazier wasn't angry. He was beyond angry.

"This is a disaster!" he said in a low, tight voice. "A

stutter—why, a stutter could hint at a congenital defect in the entire family! It could explain why Barry is handicapped!"

"I'm sorry," I said. "I'm sorry times a billion."

Jack Frazier forced himself to take a deep breath. "Well, I suppose you couldn't possibly have known it might happen."

He forgives me! How wonderful he is! "Oh, it happened to me once before, in school," I said, in a rush of relief. "I was giving a speech in seventh grade, and—"

Too late I realized that I should have kept this information to myself.

"And you didn't tell me?" As if I'd just confessed to murder. "I'd never have put you on the stand, never! I had a kid about to testify once. He stuttered out in the hall—I sent him straight home! Why didn't you tell me? Why!"

I couldn't say anything. What could I say? That I wanted to be perfect for you, Jack. Nothing less than perfect.

"You can see she's upset," Loretta said, gently. "I think all in all Ellen did beautifully—"

"Loretta, it's not for me!" Jack Frazier said. "It's for the baby!" He'd said the same thing to Aunt Beryl. "I knew how she felt. That was fine, in fact, more than fine—it put her on her best behavior. But when this kind of thing gets out of hand it's more trouble than it's worth!"

What? What kind of thing got out of hand?

"Occupational hazard?" Loretta asked, a bit sarcastically.

He blushed a little. "Usually it's the mother," he said.

I couldn't put it all together; it was as if I was listening to a language that only sounded like English. But I knew it was dreadful. This trial will destroy your family, Aunt Beryl had predicted. She was wrong. It only destroyed me.

Jack Frazier grumbled something about a phone call and left the room.

"El, don't look so forlorn," Loretta said, as we walked to our bench. I looked around for Sam, but he'd run out on me, too. "The case is as strong as ever. Nobody thinks you have a congenital defect, and Jack Frazier knows it."

She thought I was worried about the case! "Jack Frazier said something got out of hand," I said.

"He knew you had a crush on him," Loretta said softly.

I wanted to say, "But I'm Elena! You don't understand!" Instead I said, "It's not a crush. Susie Brockleman gets crushes like that, not me. Anyway Jack Frazier said he knew how I felt. He probably meant how I felt about *Barry*."

Loretta still had her arm around me; it tightened. "Did you really think he might be interested in you, Ellen?"

I shrugged. There was a guy in the art gallery, I thought, but it was too pathetic and sad to say out loud.

"Ellen, you're a pretty girl, and it's true that Jack Frazier manipulated you a little bit, probably without giving it more than a moment's thought. But he's been hired to do a job for the family. El, that's where it begins and where it ends."

I know how it began, I thought. It's the end I'm worried about.

"I want you to know something," Loretta said then. "I was so proud of you up there. Scared as you must have been, you looked Charles Friss right in the eye and said, 'Give me your worst.'"

Sam didn't come back, not even for the next witness—Dr. Simon Schlesser, who had to spell his name twice, a California obstetrician brought to New York by Jack Frazier (local doctors don't like testifying against each other). He was almost completely bald, except for a wispy fringe of hair over his ears. Don't worry, I told him in my head. I'm not exactly a tough act to follow.

"Dr. Schlesser," Jack Frazier said as the thin court reporter's eyes fluttered closed, "you have read much of the testimony in this case. Do you have an opinion as to whether or not there was malpractice?"

"I have an opinion, sir."

"Was there malpractice?"

"Yes, sir."

The language of the law—first you have to ask if the opinion exists, before you can find out what it is.

Dr. Schlesser faced the jury. "The baby's head acts as a ball valve," he said, holding up a fist. "When it's well-lodged in the pelvis, it blocks the umbilical cord. But when the head is high, not snug as a bug in a rug, there's a good chance the cord will sweep down with the water and get crushed."

"How much of a chance, Doctor?"

"Twelve percent, sir."

"Twelve percent," Jack Frazier repeated. "Dr. Niles testified there was a one percent chance."

"That's true, sir, when the head is engaged. But not when it's way up high. Then it's twelve out of a hundred."

"Tell us, what should Dr. Niles have done?"

Dr. Schlesser rubbed his head. "In medicine nobody has a crystal ball," he said. "But you have to be prepared for that *just-in-case*. How could Dr. Niles have gotten prepared? By ordering a double setup right away."

"What difference would that have made?"

Dr. Schlesser spread his arms apart, as if holding up a child. "All the difference in the world! Dr. Niles could have gotten that baby out in less than four minutes."

"Dr. Niles testified that even an emergency cesarean with everything in place takes fifteen minutes."

Dr. Schlesser shook his head. "I've done it myself a hundred times. Less than four minutes. That figure is crucial. Because after four to six minutes of oxygen deprivation, brain damage begins."

"So you are saying that Barry Gray's brain damage was preventable?"

"Most definitely," Dr. Schlesser said, looking right at the chinless redhead, who squirmed a little.

When we broke for lunch, I told Loretta I wasn't going with her to Ellen's. I need a walk, I said, but instead I just sat way off in a corner of the gray granite steps, beneath a granite-gray sky, wrapped in heat and humidity.

Ray would love hearing about this—for his book. "Ellen, stage fright! Great! Did your heart pound, your palms get sweaty?" For some reason I started thinking about "The Whole Bob Catalogue." Ray's brother, Bob, kept dozens of photo albums—all pictures of himself, with captions. In Volume IX (yes, roman numerals), there was an unfocused photo of me, Bob, and Mrs. Frost. "Ellen Gray joins us for a barbecue beneath the stars!" the caption said. Sitting on the courthouse steps, I thought, What if, when I die, that's the only record left of me, anywhere? A dark blur in "The Whole Bob Catalogue."

Out of nowhere Sam appeared on my left. "Hi," he said.

"Hi," I said back. He sat so close by, I could smell spearmint. Had he used one of those breath sprays? "Where were you? You missed some testimony."

"I needed a walk," Sam said. "Ellen, I heard what Jack Frazier said to you. He's full of crap. You just got nervous—it was so obvious to anybody with a heart."

A heart. When had Sam noticed that people had hearts? "But Jack Frazier was so upset," I couldn't help saying.

"He gets upset constantly," Sam said. "I saw him the other day, cursing nonstop when he couldn't open the trunk to his BMW." Sam handed me a brown bag. "It's an onion bagel with fresh mozzarella—and anchovies."

How did he know? I took a big bite. And swallowed. It was delicious—more delicious than anything I'd ever tasted. Sam sat there, chewing a plain bagel. Are you breaking the spell? I almost asked Sam. I'm eating, and I'm going to keep on eating from now on.

So we had our lunch date, after all.

"You looked like an adult up there," Sam said, his voice soft and direct. I could tell this was his highest possible compliment, and meant far more to him than if he'd said, "You're beautiful," or even, "I love you." Sam's eyes were dark smoky blue. He was so raw at that moment, I caught a glimpse of Sam as a tiny baby, when the world is so big and unknown, and all you know is searching, yearning.

That was when I felt it—something hard, like a baseball, circling my back. I jerked around. Suddenly Sam moved away. Sam had been rubbing my back with his fist, the hand that was always a fist.

"Thank you," I said. "Thanks a lot." But I was telling it to the steps. Sam was already gone.

fourteen

"We've met before," Charles Friss began his cross-examination of Dr. Schlesser.

I glanced behind me. Sam was sitting close to the door with his head down.

"It was at another trial, years ago," Charles Friss said. "Do you remember?"

"No," replied Dr. Schlesser.

"You had more hair. But then so did I!" Charles Friss grinned, and the chinless redhead grinned back. "Dr. Schlesser, this twelve-percent figure about the risk of a prolapsed cord—have you got it in writing anywhere?"

Jack Frazier must have anticipated this question, because Dr. Schlesser produced an article from the *American Journal of Obstetrics and Gynecology*, stating that the risk of a prolapsed cord with a high head and water broken artificially was 11.9 percent.

Charles Friss was not happy. He frowned; he paced the floor; he coughed. "All right, Doctor," he resumed, sounding almost afraid to ask the next question, "doing a double setup in this situation—have you got that in writing anywhere?"

"No, but it's good common sense—"

"That's not the point!" Charles Friss began shouting, quite relieved. "We're asking whether Dr. Niles acted in accordance with standard medical practice at Sussex Square Hospital four and a half years ago! The standard, Doctor, the standard!"

Dr. Schlesser tightened his lips. "In a situation such as Loretta Gray's, you have to be able to get that baby out fast—"

"Doctor," Charles Friss cut him off, "you claim you're such an expert on this case. Were you in the room when Barry Gray was born?"

"Unarguably, no."

"Tell me this, then. Have you testified for Mr. Frazier before?"

"Many times, sir," Dr. Schlesser answered.

"Do you think he'd keep calling you up and paying you big bucks to testify that the doctor actually did the right thing?"

Dr. Schlesser straightened his back. "Jack Frazier knows I have integrity. He trusts me to tell the truth."

Why couldn't I have been asked provocative questions like that, so that I could answer nobly, honorably?

Charles Friss grunted. "Doctor, you sound very sincere. You should get an Academy Award."

Well, Judge Patterson hit the roof on that one. "Members of the jury, you will disregard that remark," she said, "and Mr. Friss will apologize!" Then she sent everybody home early for the weekend.

Sam, it turned out, had left even earlier.

The weekend lay ahead of me like the Grand Canyon without its grandeur—a vast, hot, empty, echoing pit. I couldn't work at the gallery or visit my grandparents. On Saturday I took a long walk to nowhere, but ended up at Loretta's library. Loretta was home with Barry, but I wandered inside, anyway. Maybe I could find a book to fill up the pit a little.

I worked here after school, but none of the staff looked familiar. Upstairs on the bulletin board there was a poster of Charlie Chaplin, the man who loved much younger women. I flipped through the Subjects index, just to see what there was on Chaplin—and almost passed out. *My Life with Chaplin*, was one of the titles, by Lita Grey Chaplin.

Lita Grey. Ellen Gray. I had to have this book. It turned out I needed to go way uptown for it. I didn't care—I'd've gone out of state. And when I got it, I took it to my room to devour it.

Back and forth in my rocking chair, facing a window that looked out on a back alley, I read about how Lita Grey was fifteen when she went to work as an extra on Chaplin's film *The Kid*. At thirty-five he was already a huge star when she became "consumed by the fantasy of being held and kissed and protected by Charlie."

Lita said she first knew Charlie liked her when, scouting locations for *The Gold Rush*, he looked at her, really looked at her, and she just knew. Hadn't Jack Frazier looked at me, really looked at me, the day we met? Everyone else on the set was expected to call him Mr. Chaplin, but he encouraged Lita to call him Charlie, just as Jack Frazier had told me to call him Jack.

Don't be insane, I told myself. Jack Frazier practically admitted that you were a tactic, and nothing more! But I kept reading.

During their courtship Charlie would tell his crew, "I don't feel funny today," and then go home to meet Lita, who lied to her mother about where she was going. To keep Lita's mother happy and in the dark, Chaplin ignored Lita in public and was especially nice to the mother. In private Charlie told Lita that the whole world terrified him, but he felt comfortable with her. He said that he could pick up the phone and in five minutes any one of two thousand girls would jump into his bed, but he only wanted to be with her. And he said he loved her.

Wait a minute. Maybe Jack Frazier said what he said to throw off Loretta! So she wouldn't suspect he was falling in love with me! Maybe he had his own version of a "ban on contact." Then, once the trial was over, he would laugh and say, *Forgive me, Elena. You understand, don't you?* I kept reading.

When Lita got pregnant, Charlie turned on her and said unspeakable things to her. Lita was devastated, just as I was. Lita thought it was all over, just as I did. But it wasn't. Charlie married Lita and they had two kids.

It got ugly in the end—Lita spent a year in a mental hospital—but I didn't want to think about that. I hugged the book to my chest. *I forgive you, Jack. I understand.*

At dinner, Loretta wanted to know why I was reading a book about Chaplin, and also why I'd dashed out to Kim's Video to rent several of his movies.

"I'm studying film," I told her. "I might want to go into the movie business."

"The *silent* movie business?" she said.

The rest of that warm, muggy weekend, Barry watched the movies with me. Barry loved Chaplin and looked up at him the same way he looked at Jack Frazier. When Chaplin left a scene, even for a moment, Barry started yelling for him to come back.

Roz once told me that when you hear taped laughter on old situation comedies, it's actually people laughing at Chaplin movies. I didn't doubt it. I nearly collapsed watching *Modern Times*, where Chaplin played a factory worker who gets attacked by the boss's latest money-saving gimmick—an automated feeding machine. *City Lights* was very funny too, but the end, where a beautiful girl realizes it's the little tramp, not a millionaire, who has cured her blindness, left me soggy with tears.

Lita Grey had a scene in *The Kid*. She played a temptress, luring the little tramp. Her brown frizzy hair was pulled back, and she had large dark eyes. Barry wanted to know why I kept playing this scene over and over, and not one of the really funny ones. "Don't you think she's pretty?" I asked him.

"No," he said. Actually, he was right. She looked a bit hard.

Sunday night I returned the movies, got some groceries at Grand Union, and on my way home caught sight of Susie Brockleman, on the corner of Bleecker and LaGuardia, in front of a restaurant called Walk, Don't Walk. It looked as though Susie herself truly couldn't decide what to do—walk or not walk. When I got closer, I saw that her cheeks were splashed with tears.

"Susie, what's wrong?" I said, feeling for the first time as if we were friends. Had she fallen for yet another older man?

"Misty died!" Susie said, sobbing.

I put my arms around her shoulders. "I'm sorry," I said, feeling her whole body shake.

"Misty was sick." Susie blew her nose. "They put her to sleep. My mother wouldn't pay for the operation. She said for that kind of money I could get another dog. But I would never, never! Misty wasn't some washer-dryer that broke down. Misty was . . . I really . . ."

"Loved her," I said, and Susie nodded.

fifteen

Who sat in the witness chair Monday morning? A stormy beauty all in black–tall, slender, dark olive skin, enormous gold-brown eyes, masses of dark hair. All eyes focused on her (I seemed to be utterly invisible, at least to both Jack Frazier and Sam). She was the exact image I'd had in my head when I first heard Jack Frazier say "Elena." But the woman in the witness box said her name was Dr. Gwyneth Hunter, a pediatric neurologist.

The young, curly-haired court reporter wrote it all down, as this Elena talked in her soft, husky voice about her full professorships, and the many articles she'd written, and how she was Board certified in three separate specialties of pediatrics.

"Dr. Hunter," Jack Frazier said, "what is cerebral palsy?"

Elena cleared her throat. "*Cerebral* refers to the brain,"

she said, "and *palsy* refers to movement." With that voice she could have been telling a roomful of young men that she'd just gotten engaged. "The part of the brain that controls movement has been damaged. Symptoms vary—there may be spasms, seizures, hallucinations, hearing or speech impairment, and mental retardation. Barry Gray has ataxic cerebral palsy. His movements are poorly timed and directed, and his balance is poor."

Claire had explained all this to me years before, that no two people with cerebral palsy are exactly alike. Sam's handicaps, for instance, were only physical. There was brain damage, but nothing wrong with his mind, so to speak.

Jack Frazier said, in the language they probably taught you on your first day of law school, "With a reasonable degree of medical certainty, Doctor, could you tell us what caused Barry Gray's cerebral palsy?"

"Yes," Elena said. She looked at the jurors, who couldn't take their eyes off this movie star in their midst. "It is because of the loss of oxygen during Barry's birth. You see, cells are hungry for air. When they starve, they are destroyed. Brain cells are the first to die. Then the heart is damaged, then the retina of the eyes. Muscles take hours to die, and even after death hair might grow for a day or so."

The blonde in braids winced at that.

"Is the brain damage permanent, Doctor?"

"It is," Elena replied. "Brain cells do not recover. That is the problem with the brain." Elena sounded so confident, so sure of who she was. How did she get there?

"But Barry Gray is in therapy, Doctor," Jack Frazier said.

"Therapy helps enormously," Elena said. "For all of his life, Barry will be trying to climb a hill. Therapy helps him climb higher. Without it, he would slide right back down to the bottom."

"Doctor, is Barry Gray intelligent?"

"Intelligence," Elena began, "is the ability to learn, to reason things out, to profit from experience. IQ measures intelligence. You take the child's mental age, divide it by the actual age, and multiply that by one hundred. So if you have a two-year-old who behaves like a two-year-old, the IQ is a normal one hundred. If the two-year-old behaves more like a one-year-old, the IQ is fifty." Unlike Claire, Elena was clearly a strong believer in IQ scores. "With handicapped children, it's tricky. You have to measure their intentions. If a child tries to build a tower, it does not matter that the tower falls. That said, I believe Barry has an IQ of seventy-five, making him borderline retarded."

Retarded? Borderline retarded? I'd always known this was a possibility. But Elena was making it sound official. A couple of hours earlier, Barry had awakened all excited because he was coming to court today. His eyes were a glowing, sharp blue, his tiny palms a bit damp, and when I picked him up I could feel his heart beating fast.

"Doctor, will Barry Gray be employable?"

"No," Elena said. "His speech will never be clear enough to communicate with people properly. His hands will never write clearly. He might never understand how to work a computer, and no doubt he would have trouble with the keyboard."

Never do this, never do that. What was Elena, a gypsy with a crystal ball, a witch from Never-Never Land?

"Will Barry Gray ever marry, Doctor?"

"It is doubtful. Masturbation may be the only sexual life he will have."

I changed the subject in my head. Remember when Charlie Chaplin got so hungry in *The Gold Rush*, he boiled up his shoe for dinner? And ate it like it was a juicy steak, and the laces were spaghetti? Only it didn't seem funny to me now. I mean, his *shoe*! How desperate he must have been!

"Barry should live in a group home," Elena was saying, "with four or five other handicapped adults—and supervision, of course. But such places are expensive, and waiting lists can be ten years."

Didn't she know that Barry was going to live with me? Why didn't anybody tell her!

"How long will Barry Gray live, Doctor?"

"Children with cerebral palsy have a ninety percent life expectancy. Barry should live to age sixty-three."

But that was only . . . fifty-nine years from now. I would be seventy-five. I folded my hands. I could outlive my own baby brother. In fact, it was likely. Drops of water splashed on my hands.

During the break, Loretta rushed me past Sam, who looked near tears himself, upstairs to the ladies' room, where I couldn't stop crying.

"Mom, Barry might die when he's only sixty-three!"

"None of us has a guarantee of even that," Loretta said, holding me close.

I could feel the silk of her dress, smell her warm smell of soap and roses. It was infinitely better than the nearly overwhelming disinfectant smell; they must have mopped the walls with it. "Doesn't it upset you, Mom?"

"El, I knew it already."

My father might outlive Jack Frazier, it suddenly occurred to me. This was utterly beside the point, but it helped me stop crying.

By now Barry was waiting downstairs in the hall with Claire. "Do my eyes look puffy?" I had to ask Loretta, because there were no mirrors, and I'd forgotten my bag with its tiny mirror.

Loretta smiled. "Only a little," she said gently, which convinced me my face looked like marshmallow.

Out in the hall, Jack Frazier hovered over Barry. "Does he look handicapped enough?" he was asking Claire, who chose not to respond. "The knee pads are good. Take off the baseball cap. What about a bib, for the drooling?"

"He doesn't drool," I said.

Jack Frazier ignored me. "The white T-shirt is fine, plain and simple." He bit his thumbnail. "The red shorts are too bright—oh, never mind."

"Barry, you look terrific!" I gave him a big kiss.

"Nellie!" Barry said, breathlessly. "My here in the big building."

"Yes, you are, and I'm so happy to see you."

Jack Frazier told Claire to stay out in the hall with Barry, while Loretta and I went back to our seats.

"Dr. Hunter," Jack Frazier resumed Elena's testimony, "would it help the jury understand Barry Gray's condition if he were brought into the courtroom?"

"Yes," Elena said.

With that, Jack Frazier walked briskly across the room and opened the swinging door. Barry came bounding crookedly right in, with Claire directly behind. Once

Barry saw that all eyes were now on him, he walked more hesitantly.

"As you can see, Barry walks with an unsteady gait," Elena said.

Barry reached up to hold Claire's hand. All the jurors leaned forward—no one was going to fall asleep for this!

"May I step down?" Elena asked, doing so. There was a pad and crayon on Jack Frazier's table. "Barry, could you draw a circle for me, please?"

Barry drew a sloppy line, pressing down too hard and snapping the crayon.

"Barry, could you tell us your favorite color?"

"Blue," Barry said. It sounded like "buhhll." I heard a couple of jurors take in their breath sharply.

"Could you tell me the names of your best friends at school?"

Barry said, "Clint and Ally." It came out like "Gint nnh Aahee."

"Clint and Ally," Elena repeated, and faced the jury. "As you can hear, Barry's speech is very nasal, very difficult to understand." She turned to Barry. "Barry, would you run over to that lady at the desk, and then back again?"

Barry didn't run, exactly, but walked fast and crooked.

"His right leg turns inward," Elena said. "He can't run the way other boys can. He needs those knee pads because he falls so often."

Barry gave her a half-smile.

"Barry is cheerful," she said, smiling back. "He would have been a delightful child."

Would have been? How could she say that?

"Thank you, Barry." Elena returned to the witness stand.

Now it was time for Barry's "cross-examination."

"Hello, little man!" Charles Friss said. He had on a flashy green bow tie with red dots. He walked over to Barry and knelt down—not all the way, because his pants were a bit tight. "Could you count for me, fella, from one to five? One, two, three, four, five?"

Barry just blinked at him.

"I know you know your numbers." Charles Friss grinned. "If you don't feel like it, that's okay, buddy."

Barry thrust a finger up at the judge. "Dugh onna big-puhll," he said loudly.

Charles Friss flushed. "What?" he said.

Elena shrugged. "What was that, Barry?"

Barry repeated, "Dugh onna bigpuhll."

Everyone looked to Loretta, and she let out a little laugh. "I don't know, either," she said.

So nobody had understood but me.

"Excuse me," I said, getting up, "Barry just said, 'Duck on the big pole.' See, he's talking about the eagle on the flagpole. Barry often confuses ducks with eagles when we read picture books. Though I'm beginning to think he confuses them on purpose, to see if I'm paying attention!" As I sat down, it hit me—what had just happened. I'd spoken beautifully.

Suddenly Barry threw his arms around Charles Friss and hugged him. Everyone was absolutely stunned—and then broke out laughing.

Charles Friss had to laugh, too. "Who coached this witness?" He tried to sound playful. "I bet it was that sister of his!"

Charles Friss asked the judge to break for lunch. No doubt about it, he wanted Barry Gray out of there, fast.

Once the jury left, Jack Frazier rushed over to me and held both my hands hard. Sam was watching—I could tell without looking. "You were splendid!" Jack Frazier said. "It's totally improper to speak out at a trial, of course, but you did it marvelously, no hint of a stutter, Elena!"

I was so deeply thrilled, it could only be at the cellular level.

Jack Frazier spoke excitedly. "You realize, don't you, that Friss was trying to trick Barry with that counting business? If the jury knows what Barry's going to say, they'll understand him. Hey, why does everybody keep saying this kid can't talk right? I heard him count all the way to five! What happened couldn't have been better, Elena, not if we'd planned it that way." Jack Frazier still held my hands—way too tight, really. "Elena, the trial is tough for you, isn't it?" he asked me softly. "All those things said about Barry, about his future. Not easy for the big sister, is it?"

Jack Frazier understood me, instantly and precisely. So what if he had a dark side!

"You were just . . . perfect, Elena," Jack Frazier said, and hugged me.

sixteen

Claire and Barry joined us for lunch, and I walked all the way to Ellen's with Barry on my shoulders. Once we got there, I showed Barry the Miss Subways posters. He thought it meant these women rode the subways all day!

Barry ate french fries drenched in ketchup. "My like the man," he said of Charles Friss. "My like his ribbon."

"Yes, it was a beautiful bow tie!" I said. "Barry, you didn't mind all those people watching you?"

He shook his head.

"Barry had fun," Claire said, sounding a little surprised, cutting into an overstuffed mushroom omelet.

"My like the eagle," Barry said, grinning.

He knew! He knew an eagle from a duck! I had to hug him, though it meant getting a little ketchup on my blouse.

After lunch, Charles Friss growled, "Dr. Hunter,

you've testified for Jack Frazier before, right? Maybe a dozen times, maybe more?"

Elena shrugged. "Maybe more."

"He's taken you to lunch, that sort of thing?"

What sort of thing?

"He's taken me to lunch," Elena said casually.

Charles Friss sounded angry—jealous, maybe, that Jack Frazier got to spend time with her. Actually I didn't want to think about Elena's pre-trial consultations myself. "Dr. Hunter, you said Barry Gray is borderline retarded. Did you know that on Barry Gray's IEP two years ago his teacher said he was possibly severely retarded?"

Loretta must have known about that—she helped write these reports. No wonder none of this took her by surprise.

"I didn't see that document," Elena said. "But for many reasons children can test below their potential."

"Did you know that Barry's therapist testified that Barry might be intelligent?"

"I did not read the therapist's testimony."

"If Barry is intelligent, then he can find a job someday. You're so dead sure Barry Gray will never work."

"The therapist may have been referring to the fact that Barry understands more than he can say. Given his poor speech, I agree."

"But you said he was retarded! Stop contradicting yourself!"

"It is not a contradiction. And I said borderline retarded."

"Borderline—what a convenient word. It allows you to keep changing your mind! How can you be so sure that Barry will never marry, never have children? How can you so readily dismiss the human heart?"

This wasn't like Charles Friss. It was almost . . . poetic.

"My testimony was accurate," Elena said. "Unfortunately."

Charles Friss went on to badger her some more: How could she be so positive it was the loss of oxygen, when she didn't even know if Barry Gray was retarded or if he could find work? "In short, Dr. Hunter," Charles Friss said with a grin, "you don't know much."

And that ended Elena's testimony.

I watched Jack Frazier say good-bye to Elena, smiling and holding both her hands in his. But he'd smiled far more glowingly at me; he'd held my hands tighter. Jack Frazier and Elena weren't in love—they were only in business.

That night I took Barry to see *The Gold Rush* at Theatre 80 St. Marks, a revival movie house. The audience loved the scene where Chaplin eats his shoe. Like me, Barry got a little upset by it. "It's licorice," I whispered, something I'd learned from Lita's book.

"Don't like it," Barry said back.

"Neither did Chaplin," I said. "So for him it really was like eating a shoe!"

Lita Grey was cast to play the cruel dance hall girl in this movie, but her pregnancy forced her to quit. *The Gold Rush* was supposed to be Lita's movie, but there was another woman up there on the screen.

The last witness for our side was an economist, Dr. W. Henry Washburn (a Ph.D., not an M.D.). For his testimony Tuesday morning, he set up a blackboard and came with charts and graphs—and a pointer, even! With his burst of three-alarm-chili red hair, startlingly pale skin, black plastic glasses, and heavy lisp, he scribbled long figures with enthusiasm. "Barry Gray, at age twenty-one, will need three kinds of therapy, which costs sixty-five dollars an hour in the present day; so, allowing for inflation seventeen years from now, and assuming he finds placement in a group home, fifty thousand dollars a year in the present day. . . ." I remembered my father telling me how, as a lonely kid, he loved atoms—actually, a book about atoms. I imagined this guy as a kid, W. Henry, immersing himself with numbers, his only friends.

Then Dr. Washburn calculated what Barry, if he had gone to college, would have earned in his lifetime, from age twenty-two until retirement at age seventy. And added that to the cost of Barry's care until age sixty-three. There were so many zeros! Cost of care—over four million. Loss of earning capacity—over a million. Cost of therapy—over a quarter million. What would I have to do to take care of Barry myself, rob banks?

When Charles Friss cross-examined Dr. Washburn, he asked him, "Did you know that half of all children in this country don't go to college?"

"Yes," Dr. Washburn answered—more like "yeth."

"So how can you know Barry Gray would go to college? Maybe he'd only go to high school, or drop out. Then his earnings would be much lower."

"Barry's parents are both college educated," Dr. Washburn said, pushing up his glasses. "In such cases you can assume—"

"Exactly—assume," Charles Friss cut in. "Why don't we assume a non-college graduate working at minimum wage?"

Dr. Washburn shook his head. His skin seemed one

layer away from see-through. "We would need new projections," he said.

Charles Friss shook his head at the jury. "Dr. Washburn, you want this jury to pay for Barry Gray's lifetime care. But you also want them to pay for what he would have earned as a college graduate. Both—you want both? Barry needs care only because he has brain damage; without brain damage, he could earn his own salary. Why should this jury pay twice?"

A couple of jurors nodded very slightly at this.

Dr. Washburn didn't miss a beat. "Mr. Frazier asked me to make these computations, based on U.S. Department of Commerce statistics and the cost of health care in New York City."

Charles Friss paused. "So you're just a numbers man, is that it?"

"Exactly." Dr. Washburn grinned, exposing a huge gap in his front teeth. What he must have looked like as a kid!

Jack Frazier was on his feet before Charles Friss even sat down. "Dr. Washburn, there's no mystery here, right? These statistics are available to anyone?"

"Anyone," Dr. Washburn agreed.

"Now, if Barry Gray were a high-school instead of a college graduate, how much lower would his earnings be?"

"About twenty-five or thirty percent."

Jack Frazier sat down. "Nothing further," he said.

"I have a question," Judge Patterson said. She'd never interrupted the testimony before. "If Barry Gray didn't go to college, then he'd have four extra years of earning power. That would offset the difference somewhat." It seemed an odd thing to make a point of, considering all the hundreds of other points she might have made throughout this trial.

"Somewhat, yes," Dr. Washburn said.

"I object," Charles Friss said. "The question is irrelevant."

"Mr. Friss, I asked the question," Judge Patterson said.

"Then it's a wonderful question," Charles Friss added quickly.

Judge Patterson ignored that. "Members of the jury, the plaintiff has now called all of his witnesses. After lunch, the defense will call his first witness—"

"Your honor," Charles Friss broke in, "my first witness is Dr. Niles. He can't be here this afternoon, but, cross my heart, first thing tomorrow morning, I promise, he'll be here."

So we broke for the whole rest of the day. As soon as the jury left, Judge Patterson glared down at Charles Friss. "I must express my disapproval," she said. "This is Dr. Niles's own trial, yet he only shows up for his own testimony—and he's late even for that!"

Charles Friss coughed a bit. "Yes, your honor, I know, but he has surgery—"

"As the doctor or the patient?" she snapped.

Jack Frazier laughed his deep throaty laugh as Charles Friss grinned sheepishly.

On the walk home, Loretta seemed subdued. When I asked her why she said, "Remember, El, how upset you were by Dr. Hunter's testimony? And I said I knew it all already? Well, this was my turn. I mean, I've never cared about the salary Barry will never earn. And I don't care about money for pain and suffering, either. But Barry's care, El. I didn't know. It'll cost millions, El, millions!"

I placed my hand inside hers, and we walked along like that, holding hands.

That night we rented the movie *Chaplin*, with Robert Downey, Jr., playing Charlie. I was disappointed that in the nearly three-hour movie Lita Grey occupied *less than one minute*! Lita smiled and looked very pretty, much prettier than the real Lita, but she had no lines and Chaplin referred to her as "a deeply flawed human being."

Chaplin had a big, lush, sprawling life before and after Lita Grey. She was a blip on his screen. He was her entire screen, her only screen.

seventeen

I couldn't believe it. The benches behind Charles Friss had always been empty. Now, planted there as permanently as granite-gray steps were a middle-aged woman and a teenaged girl.

Jack Frazier leaned over me and Loretta on our bench; his forest smell was all around us. I inhaled deeply. "That's Niles's wife and daughter," he whispered.

Very softly I asked, "What are they doing here?"

"Keep your voice down! Last week Niles was here as a hostile witness. Now he's here on his own behalf. His wife came to show support—probably the girl is here because Friss wants the jury to know that Dr. Niles has a teenage girl in his corner, too."

Mrs. Niles's dark blond hair looked dandelion fragile, one gust and it would scatter. She had on a paisley silk dress, a necklace of large pearls, and thick, X-shaped gold earrings. The girl's hair was black, and so incredibly short it looked as if her head was sprinkled with pepper. She wore jeans, a tank top, and a dozen gold chains.

"They're wearing so much jewelry," I whispered. "Didn't Charles Friss tell them to tone it down?"

"Who knows?" Jack Frazier whispered back. "Maybe he did, and they didn't listen. It happens."

When the jurors filed in, they all gazed at the Niles women. And kept on looking even after Dr. Niles took the witness stand.

"Sir, you are still under oath," Hannes Leeser told Dr. Niles.

Had he been under oath all this time, then? At work, taking a shower, making love to his wife, dreaming?

"Doctor," Charles Friss began, "would you tell us, please, about your medical education?"

What followed was Dr. Niles's résumé, going as far back as college! All the residencies, certificates, internships (even a rotating one, whatever that was). The Niles women moved around a lot in their seats. I caught glimpses of their profiles—both were pretty, with large, wide-set-apart eyes, peachy skin, pencil-straight noses. Mrs. Niles slipped off her black pumps and wiggled her toes. She looked at her nails, which were long, perfectly oval, and tomato red. The girl yawned, and several minutes later yawned again. What would the jury think if she slumped over, asleep?

As Dr. Niles brought us up to the present, working at Sussex Square Hospital, the girl turned toward me. I almost gasped. She had a nose ring!

"Mrs. Gray had a proven pelvis," Dr. Niles was saying. "She'd had one child, full-term gestation, complications none."

Proven pelvis, complications none. Walter Spinak was a doctor too, but he never talked like that.

"Why didn't you order a double setup for Mrs. Gray?" Charles Friss asked.

Dr. Niles said, "Because a double setup was not the standard medical practice in Sussex Square Hospital four and a half years ago. A double setup is required only for a condition known as placenta previa, when the mother's placenta is blocking the baby's exit. Loretta Gray did not have placenta previa."

Dr. Niles explained that the water might have broken by itself, and the cord might have prolapsed while preparing for a cesarean section. "That situation would have been far worse," he said. "I would not have had my hand on the baby's head, relieving the pressure; Mrs. Gray would not have received oxygen; she would not have been in the Trendelenburg position, with her pelvis higher than her heart. Instead of a live baby we would have had a dead one."

Charles Friss rubbed his chin slowly, letting the jury chew on that a while. Dr. Niles saved Barry Gray—and now his family was suing him!

Dr. Niles went on to list all the many things that can cause cerebral palsy: the mother's smoking, drinking, or poor diet, or if she'd had an accident, or been exposed to X rays, or eaten poison, or gotten a virus or German measles, or she was too young or too old, or there was blood incompatibility between the parents, or the baby was premature, or hypoglycemic, or had brain lesions, or a head injury, or lead poisoning, or was abused.

"Wow!" Charles Friss sounded impressed. "It's a helluva list!"

Jack Frazier stretched out his long legs and gazed at the top of the flagpole.

"A loss of oxygen can also cause cerebral palsy," Charles Friss said, pacing before the jury. "Can oxygen loss occur before labor, Doctor?"

"Yes, sir. The umbilical cord can wrap itself around the baby's neck, or even around itself." And I heard him say, "Barry Gray's cord had a true not."

Not true what? Oh—*knot*. A true knot.

"A true knot forms between the third and sixth months of pregnancy," Dr. Niles went on, "when there's still room for the baby to move around. If a true knot tightens, oxygen can get cut off."

When we broke for lunch, Dr. Niles kissed his wife and hugged his daughter, whom he called Amanda. But I preferred to think of her as Nose Ring Niles.

I wanted to talk to Jack Frazier, but he was hunched over his table; his back practically had a *Don't Bother Me* sign on it. He was busier, I could see that, now that the doctor and his witnesses were testifying. Sam? Who could talk to Sam? He behaved as though we were less than strangers.

"Mom," I said, "did you know about this true knot?"

Loretta nodded. "It came up in Niles's EBT. Jack said it was a red herring—something flashy, meaningless, designed to lead you astray. Come on, let's go to Ellen's for some corned beef on rye."

"I wonder where the Niles family will have lunch. Ellen's, do you think? Will we have to share a table?"

Loretta smiled. "Not likely!" she said. "Have you ever been the enemy, El? To them, we are the enemy."

"Dr. Niles, I am quite frankly outraged!" Jack Frazier began that afternoon's cross-examination. His neck turned bright red; a vein stuck out. The curly-haired court reporter's eyes widened—she sat beneath his booming voice. "Just last week you told this jury that you had no idea why Barry Gray was brain damaged! And suddenly now you know! The knot, ladies and gentlemen, the knot! That's what happened to Barry Gray! The knot, the true knot!"

Basically Jack Frazier was having a fit.

"Is there a question?" Charles Friss demanded.

"What I want to know is," he said slowly, "which is the truth, Doctor, what you told us before, or what you're telling us now?"

"Objection!" Charles Friss yelled. "Is he calling my client a liar? What is this, the school playground?"

"Yes," Judge Patterson said. "Dr. Niles, you don't have to answer."

Dr. Niles folded his arms.

"Doctor." Jack Frazier was still at full volume, full intensity. "You don't really think the true knot caused brain damage, do you?"

Dr. Niles replied, "I said it was possible."

"Then isn't it also possible that the cord prolapse—"

"No."

"Doctor, the baby had a heart rate of fifty for eleven minutes! And he had a knot in his umbilical cord! What's the more likely cause of brain damage?"

"Objection," said Charles Friss.

"Yes, sustained," Judge Patterson said.

"Judge." Jack Frazier held out his hands. "Mr. Friss opened up this line of questioning. I'm trying to clear it up." He turned back to Dr. Niles. "Until you broke the water, the baby's heart rate was normal—all signs were normal. But the knot formed months earlier. So the baby, knot and all, was normal!"

Dr. Niles said, "We can't be sure."

Jack Frazier let out a sound of pure disgust, almost the way a kid says "yech." Then, with no notes in front of him, he proceeded to go down the entire list of the causes of cerebral palsy, knocking off each one. Doctor, did Loretta Gray get hit by a truck? Did she eat poison? Was Barry Gray abused? Was he premature? Was Loretta Gray too old? Niles made a point of saying that Barry, born two and a half weeks before the due date, was technically three days premature, and that Loretta, at thirty-five, was considered "of advanced age" for childbearing. But Jack Frazier argued that three days was hardly significant, and that a healthy thirty-five-year-old could give birth as safely as a twenty-two-year-old.

"Doctor," Jack Frazier said, exhaling deeply, "I have only one more question."

"Good!" Charles Friss belted out.

"Believe me, I'm just as happy as you are," Jack Frazier snapped.

"Please," sighed Judge Patterson.

Jack Frazier said, "Well, he's telling me how happy he is, so I'm telling him how happy I am."

"I'm sure everyone in the courtroom is happy," Judge Patterson said wearily. "Ask your question."

The juror who usually smiled to herself did not smile. This bickering was getting on her nerves.

Jack Frazier said, "You wrote 'prolapsed cord' on Barry Gray's release form. Did you mention a knot?"

Dr. Niles remained silent.

"It's not a trick question!" Jack Frazier said.

"No," Dr. Niles said.

"That is all," he said.

Charles Friss had only one more question too. "Doctor, a baby can have a normal heart rate on admission, but there could have been a slowing of the heart rate months before, and then a recovery back up to normal, right?"

"Yes, sir," Dr. Niles said.

Dr. Niles left with his wife and daughter on either arm. Amanda looked down at her flat black shoes as she walked. I watched Loretta, watching them. Was she missing my father? I could only offer her my arm. She took it.

We picked up some Chinese food for dinner, and I came home to a letter from Roz. *So drop me a line, okay?* was the P.S. *A curvy line, a crooked line—if it's a straight line, I'll follow with a joke.*

But what could I write back? Way too much had happened. *Dear Roz,* I'd have to write. *Don't get me started. Love, Ellen.*

eighteen

Dr. Bryce Ott appeared on Thursday—a pediatric neurologist, starkly, ruggedly handsome, with thick, wavy hair and a beefy build. As good-looking as Elena, the other pediatric neurologist. But his eyes were so blank, lifeless. And this man examined children? Didn't he scare them to death?

"I've seen Barry Gray," Dr. Ott told Charles Friss that rainy morning. "I've examined all his records. Barry Gray's speech is problematic but intelligible. He can walk and run. He is mildly retarded, but he may outgrow it." What? Was mental retardation a sweater? "Mind you, it's not altogether bad that Barry Gray is retarded. He'll never understand that he's different."

I had to admit, that was one way to look at it.

Charles Friss asked Dr. Ott if Barry Gray was employable.

"Yes, he can work someday, with or without college.

Perhaps in a restaurant, preparing salads, or as a typist, or as a front-desk hotel clerk."

The benches beside me were empty benches again. Where were Mrs. Niles and Amanda? Was the trial utterly behind them?

When we broke for lunch, Dr. Ott looked at me, and his gaze seemed to pierce right through my body. I shuddered all over. "Mom," I whispered, "Dr. Ott—"

"He has a glass eye," she whispered back.

Jack Frazier came over to us. "What a superb trial lawyer he'd make!"

"You liked him?" I asked, appalled.

"I liked his looks," he said. "John Wayne with a glass eye! Do I like *him*? No! Defense witnesses are whores—they take a hundred dollars and pretend they like it." He blushed. "I'm sorry," he said quietly, more to Loretta. "Elena is so mature, I forget she's a child."

"I'm not a child!" I blurted out.

"Let me phrase it another way," he said. "Witnesses like that are hired guns. They're educated up to their eyeballs—even their glass eyeballs! They earn hundreds of thousands a year, but they'll lie for a couple thousand bucks."

Wait a minute. Weren't the witnesses for our side getting paid too? Not Claire, but Dr. Washburn and Elena? But I didn't say anything.

"Did you hear the one about Barry as a front-desk clerk?" Jack Frazier said, as if it was a dirty joke. "No, I don't like Dr. Ott, and I'm going to enjoy destroying him this afternoon."

Loretta and I bought tuna-fish heros and had lunch in the park. A man with an enormous round belly passed by, and around that belly he wore a belt with shiny gold letters that said LIAR.

Loretta and I looked at each other and burst out laughing. "Mom, can you—"

"No, it's unbelievable!"

"Why would he wear something like that?" I said, doubled over.

"Maybe he's the next defense witness."

It was all we could do—laugh and laugh and laugh, as if laughter was a river and we were boats, floating helplessly on top. I hoped none of the jurors was nearby. How would it look?

"Are you getting paid for your testimony?" Jack Frazier asked Dr. Ott that afternoon.

"I certainly hope so," Dr. Ott said, jutting out his strong, square chin. "I almost got run over by a cab just now."

"A near miss, Doctor?" It didn't mean anything, but sounded as if it did. "Doctor, have you heard Barry Gray speak?"

"Barry Gray did not speak during our consultation." Why didn't this surprise me? "But I have seen written reports of his speech."

"And on that basis you have Barry Gray working as a front-desk clerk in a hotel?"

Dr. Ott crossed his legs. "I said it was a possibility."

"Doctor, the jury heard Barry Gray speak; you have not. But you are telling them that Barry Gray could greet guests, book reservations, answer the phone? Hotels are concerned with image and speedy service, Doctor. What hotel would hire Barry Gray?"

"I did not say he was employable now. We are talking about many years in the future."

Jack Frazier put his hands on his hips, as if to scold a child. "What boss, even a good-hearted one who wanted to hire the handicapped, would take on a typist who typed slowly, clumsily, with many errors? Yes, I'll take Barry Gray, never mind about efficiency and accuracy?"

Dr. Ott cleared his throat. "Perhaps Barry Gray could work tying up boxes in a sheltered workshop."

"Doctor, are you aware that Barry Gray may never be able to tie his shoes? You said Barry Gray could run. The jury saw that he could not."

"Perhaps he did not feel like running in the court-room."

"You said it was a good thing Barry Gray is retarded, because he'll never know he's different. Doctor, Barry Gray already knows. You may assume his therapist testified to that. His teachers at UCP put it in writing. He knows, Doctor, he knows he's a big boy and still in diapers. And years from now he'll be an even bigger boy still in diapers! His frustration—"

"His frustration comes from something else," Dr. Ott broke in.

"Oh?" Jack Frazier stretched out that "Oh?" filling it with sarcastic disbelief.

"Barry Gray has been taught Sign language. I believe this is terribly confusing to him—the language of the deaf mixed in with the language of the hearing."

The chinless redhead looked impressed.

Jack Frazier was silent a moment and hung his head.

"Doctor," he said softly, "are you telling this jury that Barry Gray is so retarded he'll never know he's different, but not retarded enough to keep him from working in a hotel? That he's frustrated not because he can't walk or talk properly, but because he knows a dozen words of Sign language?"

Dr. Ott bristled. "Don't twist my words, counselor. You're dealing with an intelligent person, perhaps as intelligent as you. I have a worldwide reputation—children from all over come to me."

"Doctor, I was only repeating—"

"I cannot answer your question the way you are proposing it."

Jack Frazier seemed incredulous. "That's your answer?"

"I cannot answer your question," Dr. Ott repeated.

There was silence, until Judge Patterson said, "That is his answer. Continue, Mr. Frazier."

It got worse. Every time Jack Frazier asked Dr. Ott something, he said he couldn't answer, or the question must be reworded, or Jack Frazier was deliberately confusing the jury. Finally Dr. Ott, furious, said, "You've never been in a doctor's office except as a patient. I can't answer your stupid, stupid questions!"

So Jack Frazier made a grand sweeping gesture of his arms and declared, "Then I don't have another question of you, sir, for the rest of this trial."

That night I dreamed Jack Frazier and I were married, living in the loft with Barry. The three of us were sitting down to dinner; on the kitchen table there was a huge, shiny pot with a shiny lid. I could even see our distorted reflections in it. Jack Frazier proudly lifted the lid, and inside the pot was—a boiled shoe.

Occasionally on television I see a news item about a wild

animal that shows up in somebody's suburban backyard: a small brown bear, a fox, a bobcat. There's a special look in the animal's eyes when it's cringing and caught in a too-small wire cage in front of bright lights and a TV camera.

It was the exact look in the eyes of the last defense witness: Dr. Janet Underwood, an obstetrician. She was short, with gray curls that circled her head. The dark tweed suit she wore should have been on a hanger at home, waiting for weather that was forty degrees cooler.

"People must understand a reality of medicine," Dr. Underwood said, so softly that Judge Patterson had to ask her to speak louder. "Things can go wrong even when the doctor is not negligent. This is called maloccurrence. It's a turn for the worse due to circumstances beyond the control of the most skillful and caring doctors."

Charles Friss nodded vigorously. "Maloccurrence," he said approvingly, as if she'd gotten it right at the spelling bee. "Now, Doctor, when a baby is in the womb, before they eat meat and potatoes and get fat like me, basically feeding is just fluids, right?"

"Fluids and nutrients, yes. Problems can crop up here, too. There's a defect in tooth enamel in many babies with cerebral palsy. Tooth enamel forms during the last six months of pregnancy. This could hint at a hormonal imbalance in the mother, or an undetected infection, or a congenital defect."

I swallowed hard.

"Do you think Dr. Niles acted within the standard of care?" Charles Friss asked her.

"Yes, sir. He took all the proper steps to relieve the baby's distress—he leaned the mother back, he gave her oxygen, he lifted the baby's head off the cord. But the baby's heart rate did not return to normal; the baby did not behave the way a normal baby should. That is why I believe this baby was brain damaged before he ever got to the hospital."

Charles Friss looked thoughtful. I could see several jurors considering this possibility too.

For lunch Dr. Underwood sat outside the courtroom on a bench by herself, crossing her legs at the ankles and eating a banana. As far as I knew, she sat there the whole time. I saw her as Loretta and I left for Ellen's, and again when we got back. It made me a little sad, to see her alone like that, without even Charles Friss for company. She looked like someone I might just start talking to, if she'd wandered into Cave instead of this trial.

Jack Frazier began his cross-examination. "So you're saying Barry Gray's brain damage was unavoidable."

"Yes—well, yes." Again Judge Patterson had to remind her to speak up.

"What you're saying, Doctor—it's like chalk and cheese. Did Barry Gray come to Sussex Square Hospital with brain damage, or did he get brain damage once he was there?"

Dr. Underwood shook her head. "Chalk—cheese?"

"Yes, Doctor! Chalk and cheese! Chalk is one thing and cheese is another!"

"You mean like apples and oranges," Dr. Underwood said. "I didn't understand—"

"Could I get an answer to my question?" Jack Frazier thundered at her.

Dr. Underwood shrank even further inside herself.

"Doctor, does Loretta Gray have a hormonal imbalance? Does Barry Gray have defective tooth enamel?"

"Not that I know of, sir."

"What proof is there, then, of preexisting brain damage?"

"There might be an unknown cause, sir. We might never know."

"How convenient!" Jack Frazier yelled. "Just like your diagnosis of 'maloccurrence'! Doctor, if Barry Gray had been delivered by cesarean section anytime during the three hours that Dr. Niles remained in his office, could Barry Gray have avoided serious injury?"

"I cannot answer that," Dr. Underwood said. "The cesarean section was not called for. You are inventing a situation— It's impossible to— I'm sorry, I'm not used to being cross-examined. It's my first time."

If I were Jack Frazier, I wouldn't strike out at this witness too much. Dr. Underwood was nail-biting nervous, but her testimony sounded sincere. Sometimes you could see beyond the fraction—she wasn't a hired gun, to use his more polite term.

But he didn't back off. "Doctor, why did Loretta Gray deliver her baby in a hospital and not at home? To be in a place that could handle emergencies!"

"But there was no emergency," Dr. Underwood said.

"The risk, Doctor, the risk! If you read the testimony, you'd know—a twelve-percent risk!"

In her meek way, Dr. Underwood held her ground. "Dr. Niles did what any good doctor should have done under the circumstances. When things go wrong, it's tragic, but it's nobody's fault."

Jack Frazier sat down with a loud, bored sigh.

Charles Friss coughed for a bit, took pills, drank water, and announced, "Defense rests."

"All right, everybody," Judge Patterson faced the jury, "take a deep breath." The chinless redhead was the only one who visibly did so. "We've reached a milestone. Now all we have left are the summations and my charge. Have a good weekend—and remember, don't discuss the case."

"Us, too, El," Loretta whispered. "Let's have a good weekend and not discuss the case!"

Actually we had a great weekend. We took Barry to the Central Park Zoo and watched polar bears swim. At a playground on Mercer Street, we chased Barry around a sprinkler, spraying water all over his thin arms, legs, and torso. We watched *The Wizard of Oz*. And we talked about Daddy.

"Everyone has to be super quiet on a submarine," I told Barry, "so enemy subs can't find you. Every bathroom has a sign that says, *Shh! Don't drop that seat!*"

Barry laughed.

We wrote Robert a twenty-word familygram, telling him we missed him; that we couldn't wait to see him in a couple of weeks; and that it was hot, very hot. In other words, we told him a fraction—a fraction that a censor could swallow whole.

nineteen

Monday morning again—the trial was now exactly two weeks old. Outside, the sun blazed. Inside, it was cool, bright; the air conditioner hummed; the clock had developed a buzz; I could feel Loretta's rayon dress against my knee; Sam was still stuck in his silence; and I realized that this place didn't feel like a home away from home, but more like a life away from my life.

It took Charles Friss forever to begin his summation. He coughed, frowned at his notes, and paced slowly, thoughtfully, before the jury. Finally he said, "Thank you, ladies and gentlemen, thank you. I can't thank you enough! Thank you for being here. Thank you for paying attention. Thank you for"—he cupped his ear—"listening." Then he yelled, "My hat is off to Jack Frazier! He did his best to win your sympathy. But I have the facts on my side!"

Charles Friss repeated things Dr. Niles had said, backed up by things Dr. Ott and Dr. Underwood said. "Brilliant, my witnesses were brilliant. Jack Frazier's witnesses were—how can I put this? Not so brilliant. Take Gwyneth Hunter. Every time you see Jack Frazier, Gwyneth Hunter shows up. Makes you wonder, doesn't it? Claire Withers Stonehill—what was that all about? Opinions! That and a token will get you on the subway!"

Gently, softly, Charles Friss added something different, something new: "Let's just say, if there's a congenital defect in a family member, let's just say—for the sake of argument, now—the defect is a stutter. Well, that might indicate a genetic abnormality, which might then show up in a second child."

So, the seed was planted. Would it take root and flower? The chinless redhead, in pearl button earrings, nodded.

Charles Friss continued, "Mr. Frazier will raise his booming voice—and he gives me a headache, how about you?—and ask for totally absurd numbers. Double-digit millions! And he'll expect you to cut that in half, to just a handful of millions. Know what I think?" He thumped the rail. "That's"—*thump!*—"out"—*thump!*—"rageous!" Then Charles Friss whispered, as if lulling a baby to sleep: "Don't be fooled, dear members of the jury. Don't let the persuasive Jack Frazier persuade you that there was wrongdoing here. He has invented a standard of care—this double setup—and he has asked you to swallow it. Don't. The double setup wasn't the standard of care at Sussex Square Hospital four and a half years ago, and it isn't the standard of care today. Never do harm to anyone, says the Hippocratic oath, the oath all doctors take. My client, Dr.

Warren Niles, has been true to that oath. Thank you, members of the jury, thank you." Charles Friss bowed deeply. I half expected applause.

Judge Patterson asked if the jury needed a break (Charles Friss had spoken for only fifteen minutes). I could see the chinless redhead squirming, but like everybody else she said no.

"May it please the court," Jack Frazier began. "Ladies and gentlemen of the jury." And he clicked into an altogether different person—fully animated, arms gesturing this way and that, talking to all parts of the room. "This case is about negligence and carelessness and callousness," he told the ceiling. "This is about a woman with no trouble in her pregnancy," he turned to us, "entering a hospital with a baby about to be born, a perfect, normal baby with a perfect, normal heart rate. But there were complications—high head, water not broken. So what did Dr. Warren Niles do? He went to his office for three hours." Jack Frazier faced the witness chair. "Before breaking the water, Doctor, why didn't you prepare a cesarean section? Such things are not done, the doctor replied. But Doctor, you knew there might be an emergency. You knew, Doctor, you knew! Why did you do nothing to prepare for a tragedy that did in fact occur?" Jack Frazier turned to the jury. "He knew, ladies and gentlemen, yet he did nothing. We're talking about getting a few people together to do a cesarean section, not calling in the Army and the Navy and the National Guard. A few people, against the risk of brain damage and death. The glory of medicine is to anticipate problems and to deal with them. But for Loretta Gray there was no anticipation, no preparation, no caring." Jack Frazier circled the floor;

his face darkened, reddened. "And what about those three hours, Doctor? Paperwork, he replied. I submit to the jury that Dr. Niles may have been doing something else, but even if it was paperwork, could any piece of paper be more important than Loretta Gray's baby, a time bomb waiting to go off? Barry Gray's heart rate plunged to fifty. That low heart rate—the baby's way of screaming, *I'm in trouble!* Only then did Dr. Niles order a cesarean section. But it was too late. Far too late. Is that acceptable to you, members of the jury? Send a message to Sussex Square Hospital that you will not accept it!"

Already Jack Frazier had spoken longer than Charles Friss.

"Are you going to accept Dr. Ott, who had Barry Gray working as a front-desk clerk at a hotel? What hotel? What century? What planet? Did that have the ring of truth? Are we to believe Dr. Underwood? She had the perfect answers—*maloccurrence* and *unknown*. Whatever caused Barry's problems—some bad luck, is all. Oh, thank you, Doctor—case is over! Let's all go home!" Jack Frazier threw some papers into his briefcase and snapped it shut. And smiled. "We know, don't we, that Barry Gray choked for eleven minutes. But no, Dr. Underwood insisted, he was already handicapped. With a normal pregnancy and a normal heart rate, Doctor? A baby with a perfect head, eyes, face, body, hands, toes—and an imperfect brain? What is your proof? Now I will remind you of how truly desperate the defense is, how you could see through their arguments with the worst cataracts. That red herring—the knot in the cord. They brought it up, why not give it a fitting burial? Dr. Niles claimed at his first appearance that he didn't know why Barry was brain damaged. But a week later, he knew: the knot in the cord! Does this have the ring of truth? Ladies and gentlemen, it's this simple—if a cesarean section had been in place, Barry Gray could have gotten out of his mother's body in three or four minutes." Jack Frazier looked at the jury, long and hard. Several jurors straightened their shoulders. "Does Loretta Gray seem like a liar? Is she crazy? Or is she a devoted mother trying to put back the broken pieces of her son's life? Ellen Gray, her daughter, got a little nervous on the witness stand. Understandable? Perfectly. A congenital defect? In a pig's eye!"

I straightened my shoulders too.

"Ladies and gentlemen, you remember Dr. Hunter's testimony. Barry Gray will never work, never marry, never care for a family of his own. His cerebral palsy affects every single aspect of his life—a shortened life—and every day taken away was denied him by a doctor's negligence." Jack Frazier made a fist, and the chinless redhead flinched. "What is the most frustrating thing on this earth? Not to be understood. What kind of life lies ahead for Barry Gray? A life of frustration. Is this pain and suffering? If it isn't, I don't know what is! You have the opportunity to give something back, to compensate Barry for his pain and suffering, for his care, for the salary he will never earn. Of course, no money will make Barry Gray whole again. Such things are forever beyond the powers of lawyers or doctors." And Jack Frazier asked the jury for seventeen million dollars.

I couldn't help it—it bothered me that he didn't mention that his firm would take one third of the money. But I guess this was another one of those things that simply didn't come up.

"Members of the jury, soon you will leave the court-house and return to your own lives. The memory of Barry Gray will be fresh. Weeks will pass, and you may think of Barry Gray now and then. Months will pass, and years, and you may remember Barry Gray only very occasionally. Please feel, now and forever, that when you had the one and only chance to do it, you did justice for Barry Gray."

Jack Frazier had spoken nonstop for forty-five minutes.

During the break I rushed over to him. "Jack, your summation! It was so . . . accurate." Why couldn't I express myself better? Because it was so much more than accurate. It was a plea for Barry's life.

"Thank you, Elena." For the first time, Jack Frazier looked tired, those spectacular brown-green eyes sur-rounded by tiny red lines. "That makes me feel better. At the end of a trial there's—how shall I say it? A sense of loss."

This is not the end, I wanted to tell him. Not this time.

After the break it was Judge Patterson's turn. We heard more from her than we had during the whole trial. "There is no magic formula here," she began. "Members of the jury, you must decide whose testimony you believe. Keep in mind a witness's appearance, manner, age." Age? Was that a reference to me? "You must ask yourself, does a witness have an interest in the outcome? Even so, that person may be telling the truth. You may believe only part of someone's testimony, or almost all of it. It is up to you. You accept and reject. You believe and disbelieve. *You.*" All the jurors were listening carefully—soaking it up, really. "You must not be affected by sympathy, or by whether your verdict will be popular or unpopular, or if it will help or hurt anyone. You must deal only with the facts. The burden of proof is on the plaintiff. This means that the evidence you find believable must weigh more heavily on the plaintiff's side. If the evidence is equal on both sides, you must find for Dr. Niles. You may have heard the term 'beyond a reasonable doubt.' That applies only to criminal court."

Judge Patterson looked at each juror. She wasn't nearly as intense as Jack Frazier, but intense in her own way. "Five out of six of you must agree on a verdict. Five out of six must agree on the answers to the questions on your verdict sheet. Did Dr. Niles depart from good and accepted medical practice? If no, report your decision. If yes, proceed to question two. Was this departure the cause of Barry Gray's brain damage? If no, report your decision. If yes, go on to question three. Here you can award Barry Gray money. If the answer is 'none,' write 'none.' The case is in your hands. Listen to each other. Change your minds if reason and logic so dictate." Judge Patterson stood, tall in her dark robe, and opened the oak door behind her. "Lunch has been ordered, and Mr. Leeser will get you anything else you need. The two alternates must remain here while the other six jurors retire for their deliberations."

"Well," Loretta said as the six left the room, "that, as they say, is that."

Judge Patterson spoke to the two alternates—the guy in the Gap ad and the blonde in braids. I heard the guy say, "Can't we stay for the verdict?"

"It could take days," Judge Patterson told him with a grin. "And nobody decides anything before lunch."

Sam had come prepared—with a thick book. Loretta chatted with Sheila. Hannes Leeser had left with the jurors. And I sat on my bench with absolutely nothing to do.

"This waiting—it's the second-worst time," Jack Frazier told me, frowning, fine lines around his mouth.

"What's the first-worst time? I mean, the worst time."

"When the jury sends a note saying they have a verdict. There's about fifteen minutes before you actually hear what it is. It's an eternity."

"So, can't we just . . . relax?"

"Relax! I take my hat off to you if you can relax!"

Jack Frazier spoke to the alternate jurors while Charles Friss sat at his table and read a newspaper. Afterward, Jack told me, "There's a superstition—when the alternates are for you, it's the kiss of death."

"They were for us?"

"Split. Let's take that as a good sign. The man was for us all the way. He said he felt like such a part of things, he was so unhappy about missing the deliberations. The woman was completely at sea. I remember her from the *voir dire*—she's all mixed up! No idea what she wants to do in life. She'll drift, always drift."

I could see that for Jack Frazier this was the absolute worst way to be. No need to worry. I was the exact opposite of a drifter.

twenty

Jack Frazier couldn't sit still. He roamed the echoing circular halls, and paced the room, and occasionally sat in a juror's seat, jiggling his foot. Charles Friss stayed at his table, reading newspapers thoroughly. I even saw him scanning the classifieds!

Suddenly Jack Frazier burst out with, "Elena! Have lunch with me!"

I said yes, oh, yes, that sounds wonderful. I didn't say that Loretta and I had arranged to meet Maribeth at Ellen's. Posters of Miss Subways weren't Jack Frazier's style, were they?

But we didn't leave right away. He seemed to be waiting for something—but what?

I got my answer. A dark-haired, dark-eyed woman in a star-white sleeveless dress swept into the room and kissed him. Just like that! I was about to get volcanically jealous until I saw the wedding ring. So, she wasn't his girlfriend. She was his married sister, or his married cousin, or his married friend—

Jack Frazier said, "This is Kay, my wife."

She was his married wife?

Maybe I hadn't heard him correctly. "Your wife?" I said carefully, waiting for him to laugh his deep throaty laugh and say, "Wife? Did I say *wife*? Kay is my accountant."

"Married twelve years next Friday," Kay said, and hugged his arm.

Loretta was there too, shaking Kay's hand and smiling at her.

Still I couldn't believe it. "But Jack, you're not wearing a ring!"

"Many men don't," Jack Frazier said, clearly uncomfortable. "Kay, Ellen is joining us for lunch."

Oh, so I was the one joining *them*. And now I was "Ellen"!

"How nice," Kay said, and smiled. She was pretty, run-of-the-mill pretty, the kind of pretty you see in commercials for paper towels.

"I'm meeting a friend at Ellen's coffee shop," Loretta said. "Why don't we all go together?"

Sure, why not? Bring Sam, too, while you're at it! Luckily he wasn't around to be asked.

Married. Jack Frazier was married. But he didn't seem married! On the way to Ellen's Loretta poked me in the arm—*what's with you?* I tightened my body into itself.

Inside Ellen's, Maribeth was waiting. Her hair was loose and extra frizzy, and she wore her brown-orange-red, accordion-pleated dress. "Did you win yet?" she asked.

"No," I said sharply, but everyone else laughed. She was kidding.

We all sat at a rectangular table for five—*five!*, when it was supposed to be two. On the wall behind Kay was the Miss Subways who was Ellen herself. *Ellen has appeared in school plays and plans to pursue an acting career.* We ordered sandwiches. Crab meat salad for me.

"Does the tuna salad have celery?" Maribeth asked, scrunching up her nose at the waitress, who told her yes, and onion. "Oooh, onion!" Maribeth grinned. "I suppose I can live with the celery. Story of my life. I want onion and get stuck with celery, too."

Maribeth could have been talking about anything, or nothing even, but I knew she was talking about Sam.

"Where did you two meet?" Loretta asked Mr. and Mrs. Jack Frazier.

"At Fordham Law," Kay said, placing a hand on her husband's. Lita Grey must have felt this way watching the dance hall girl in *The Gold Rush. That's supposed to be me!*

"You're a lawyer too?" Loretta asked.

"Not a trial lawyer," Kay laughed. "Corporate." She was always laughing—probably an utterly shallow person who couldn't understand the dark side of life the way I did, the dark side of Jack Frazier.

Our lunch arrived. Jack Frazier had ordered a bacon cheeseburger and french fries. "Kay got me to switch sides," he said. "I started out with an insurance company, but Kay convinced me that throwing injured people out of court without compensation wasn't exactly palatable."

So he wasn't always on the side of the underdog. Jack Frazier was who he was in part because of Kay, his wife.

"Do you have children?" Loretta said.

"We have two daughters," Jack Frazier said. "Chloe is nine, and Beatrice is six."

"*Seven,*" Kay said, laughing again.

I sank into my chair. It was slightly padded but felt like cast iron. Two daughters! Everybody at the next table had ordered overstuffed omelets, and the smell of maybe a dozen eggs drifted over to us.

"You're so quiet," Jack Frazier said to me, and I just shrugged. *I have a boyfriend,* I thought, to console myself. But Ray felt so far away, a lot farther away than Vermont. It was as if he'd moved, leaving no forwarding address.

"Sam's been telling me about the trial," Maribeth said to the Fraziers. "Loretta and Ellen know my relationship with my son is a bit rocky. But this trial has turned us into friends, something I never dared imagine!"

That was Maribeth—opening up to Kay, a total stranger. It was as bad as Barry hugging Charles Friss.

"Sam's been terrific," Loretta said.

"What's so terrific about sitting in the back of a room?" I burst out, my mouth full of crab meat salad. That time on the courthouse steps was so unusual, it almost didn't count.

"Sam's shown us unbudging support," Loretta explained, "and hasn't gotten in our way, either."

I figured that was one way to look at it. You could also say that Sam was a Peeping Tom.

"I can remember when Sam and I started having trouble," Maribeth said, as if someone had specifically asked her this. "Sam was seven. I had to run a quick errand, so I told Sam to wait for me at my gallery. Stay on the stoop, I told him, don't move. Well, when I got back, there was the stoop, and no Sam. I was frantic. Where was he? I ran and ran, and finally found him, running on the street, hysterically crying. 'Why were you running?' I asked him. He said, 'Looking for you, looking for you.' The look in his eyes. He was so . . . so . . . how can I describe it?"

"Raw," I heard myself say, remembering the court-house steps.

"Exactly!" Maribeth slapped the table.

That afternoon—still waiting, waiting, waiting. Jack Frazier was pleasant to me and called me Elena. Apparently he saw nothing wrong with being a married man with two daughters. I didn't know what to think. So I emptied out my head, like water from a tub. All that was left was cold, white porcelain and the dark smudge of a ring.

Just before three o'clock the jury wrote a note. No verdict, not yet—they wanted to hear some testimony read back. Loretta's account of Barry's birth, and Dr. Niles's explanation of why he didn't order a double setup.

"Elena, it's good they asked for Loretta's story," Jack Frazier told me. "Not so good about Dr. Niles. Usually the jury wants to hear again the person they believe more strongly."

So we all sat in our usual seats as the thin court reporter read back the testimony, repeating in a fast, flat monotone things Loretta had said with great emotion. It was like the world's worst acting.

At the end of the day, still no verdict, and the jury went home for the night.

When I got home, I found a letter from Ray. *Still need a title for my book,* he wrote. *But you know what? I have one for my next book! Here's the idea. The book will be one long, twisty question. Want to know the title? "Good Question."* I read the whole letter, even the P.S.: *I'm dedicating my book to you, Ellen. Not "Good Question"—the other one.*

When I saw Ray, I could tell him I'd come up with a title for his first book—*Don't Get Me Started*. I could see Ray smile. "Not bad, Ellen! Not bad for a story that goes on forever." But I also had to tell him we were breaking up. I'd liked Ray because he never cluttered up my head. And now it was all over, for just that reason. I could see the smile disappear.

The next morning the sky was a drizzly, dull gray. We sat around and sat around. This waiting, it wasn't like waiting for a bus. It was like when you were a kid and couldn't wait to be a teenager.

Out of nowhere Judge Patterson announced, "I'll be in my chambers."

I was just so restless. "Can I come with you?" I blurted out.

I could see Judge Patterson about to say no, but hesitate. "For just a moment," she said.

I followed her through the oak door, the one the jury always used. On the other side was a dim, narrow hallway with a series of closed oak doors. One door must belong to the jury. Another was clearly marked HON. EVELYNNE PATTERSON.

Her chambers were small but warm: dark, rich, red carpeting and curtains, knotty-wood paneling, and thick, leather-bound books on bookshelves from floor to ceiling. The smell of strong coffee was everywhere; I saw a coffee machine dripping away. Judge Patterson sat at a large desk with piles of papers. I sat across from her, on a yellow upholstered chair that looked soft but was actually quite firm.

Judge Patterson smiled gently. "It's decaf," she said. "Want some?"

I shook my head. This was a little intimidating, like getting summoned to the principal's office, even though I'd just invited myself in.

"What's life like for you, outside of the courtroom?" Judge Patterson asked, as if she really wanted to know.

"Fine," I replied. "I play with Barry, go to the movies, take walks, things like that." I hoped I didn't sound like I was in the witness chair.

Judge Patterson cleared her throat. "Outside of the trial altogether, I meant. Your *real* life."

"Oh." I felt my cheeks grow warm. "Real life is, well, it's—busy."

She raised an eyebrow. "Too busy?" she said.

"No. I mean, it sounds busy. In school, I'm captain of the softball team and in charge of the recycling center. After school I work part-time at my mother's library, and at an art gallery on the weekends, and I help out with Barry, some."

Judge Patterson was silent a moment. Her forehead looked smooth as glass. "That is busy," she said casually, but I knew what it sounded like to her. Too busy, after all. How could I tell her it was for Barry?

"What do you think of our legal system?" Judge Patterson asked me then.

I shrugged. "It's okay."

"It's not," Judge Patterson said, with that gentle smile. "But it's the best we've got."

"I like Jack Frazier." I couldn't believe I'd told her this. I was as bad as Maribeth!

"He's a fine lawyer," she said, as if that was what I'd

meant. "So is Charles Friss. They're very different, of course." I was glad she'd noticed! But what she said next made me think she still lumped them together: "Jack Frazier is fiery and loud—I'd like to see him lower the volume. Charles Friss is folksy, like a relative. But both men are reliable and honest."

I said, "How can both be honest, when somebody's lying?"

"Good point!" Judge Patterson laughed. "Let's just say that each believes in what he is representing." She pushed up her glasses and studied me closely. "You're much older than Barry. Twelve years, a whole childhood. I think it's harder on the sibling when the handicapped child is older. That child gets all the care and attention, and the younger child gets lost. Where is her childhood?"

I gave her a little nod. Was she talking about herself? I wondered. A little girl who became a Supreme Court judge?

"You're at the age now when you're looking into the future, am I right? You'll be Barry's guardian someday. That will keep you busy too. Even with Barry living outside the home."

I'd never heard it labeled like that—Barry's guardian. A knight on a white horse. "Barry will live with me," I told her.

Almost as an aside Judge Patterson said, "If Jack Frazier wins this case, in the long run you'll benefit more than anyone."

"But it's for Barry," I said, confused. "It's Barry's case—"

"It's for you," Judge Patterson insisted. She stood up. Clearly my visit was over.

Barry's case—wasn't it Barry's case? What was she saying? That it was my case. Ellen's case.

I was a bit stunned as I joined Loretta on our bench, where she was flipping through a magazine.

"Mom, I was just talking to the judge—"

"She's a lovely woman," Loretta broke in. She had a blue scarf around her neck, and her hair looked like yellow silk. "We could've gotten so unlucky, El. The judge could have been hell on wheels—"

"Mom, she said this case—it's for me. If we win. It's for me."

"But this trial has always been for you, El," Loretta said simply.

Now I was doubly stunned. There was no air in my voice when I told her, "You never said so."

Loretta wrapped her arm around me. She smelled like soap and roses. "For so long, you didn't even want to talk about the trial," she said. "Remember? Anyway, I wasn't sure you'd believe me."

This sounded so familiar. Glinda, in *The Wizard of Oz*, telling Dorothy only at the very end she could go home simply by clicking her heels. Dorothy, too, had wanted to know why Glinda hadn't mentioned this crucial little bit of information right away. "You wouldn't have believed me," Glinda, too, had said.

"But I want Barry to live with me!" I said.

Loretta give me a firm little shake. "That was never acceptable to me or Robert."

Never acceptable? "But I want Barry," I pleaded.

"El, you can want Barry and he can still become a burden to you. If you live your whole, entire life around him, that's what will happen."

I settled into her silky hair, into the soapy, rosy smell. And knew what it was I'd been scared of for so long. That Barry would eclipse my life, the one that hadn't even started yet, my life as an adult. And that I'd have to make my way in that darkest place of all, the shadow of the eclipse.

Afraid of the dark, at my age.

Suddenly Hannes Leeser called out, "We have a verdict!"

twenty-one

An eternity, Jack Frazier had called these fifteen minutes. Loretta and I sat quietly on our bench, obedient as A-plus students who did loads of extra credit.

The jury came in, expressionless as park statues. Good sign? Bad sign?

"Has the jury agreed on a verdict, Madam Forelady?" Hannes Leeser called out.

"It has," said the woman who looked like Loretta.

I almost wished the clock would stop, this time for real. What was on the other side of this moment?

Hannes Leeser said, "As to question number one, did Dr. Niles depart from the standards of good and accepted medical practice in not having set up for an immediate cesarean section before breaking the waters of Mrs. Gray—how does the jury respond, yes or no?"

"Yes," she said.

Yes. She said *yes.*

"Was it unanimous?" Hannes Leeser said.

"Yes."

So it was yes—even from the chinless redhead!

"As to question number two, was the departure the proximate cause of Barry Gray's brain damage—how does the jury respond, yes or no?"

"Yes," she said.

"Was that unanimous?"

"Yes."

"As to question number three, state the amount you have determined for pain and suffering—"

"Five million dollars."

"Custodial care and loss of earnings—"

"Six million dollars."

"Did you total these figures?"

"We did, sir. Eleven million dollars."

Loretta let out a gasp. Or maybe it was me.

"Were those unanimous, those figures?"

"Yes."

Eleven million dollars! Eleven . . . eleven . . . this number echoed in my head. Because I'd heard it throughout the trial—loss of oxygen for eleven minutes. Barry got a million dollars for every one of those minutes!

Eleven million dollars. For Barry. For me to help Barry. For *me.*

I heard somebody crying softly. Maybe it was me, gasping and crying and not feeling it. But the sound came from the back of the room.

Sam.

"Do you wish to poll the jury?" Judge Patterson asked.

"Yeah," Charles Friss said, sounding tired.

Poll the jury? Did that mean ask if they were Democrats or Republicans? No, it did not. Hannes Leeser called out each juror's full name and asked if he or she agreed on this final verdict. Each one said yes.

"I want it on the record," Charles Friss said defiantly. "I will appeal!" And let out a hearty cough.

And suddenly it was over, just as Hannes Leeser had said it would be. Judge Patterson thanked the jury. "I hope perhaps we will work together someday," she said. "With you as jurors, of course."

Judge Patterson said that now the jurors could talk to the lawyers or anyone else. "But don't discuss what went on in the jury room," she said. That experience, I guessed, belonged only to them.

Jack Frazier greeted the jurors as they stepped down from the jury box, thanking them warmly.

"They believed us, El," Loretta whispered. "Isn't it wonderful?"

I agreed.

The jury gathered around me and Loretta like kids around a sprinkler.

"We all admired your family so much," said the woman who looked like Loretta, in a slight Southern drawl. "We just fell in love with Barry!"

The man with the spiky gray hair grinned at me. "You were very brave," he said.

I looked around for the chinless redhead; she was the only one who'd left.

"What did you talk about?" I asked. "When the trial was going on, I mean."

Several of them laughed.

"The lawyers," said the woman who wore colorful

headbands. "Pat had us in stitches. She did a perfect Mr. Frazier."

This I had to see.

It turned out Pat was the Loretta look-alike. She took a step back, furrowed her eyebrows, and said in a rather deep, loud voice, "It's like chalk and cheese—chalk is one thing and cheese is another!"

Amazing. She'd captured him exactly. Jack Frazier laughed, but he seemed taken aback. Couldn't he joke about himself?

"Now Friss! Do Friss!" said the woman with the headband.

Pat slouched, shrugged, smiled lazily. "What can I tell you?" she said. "I don't feel so hot. But I'll be okay."

I looked around for Charles Friss, but he was gone too. And so was Sam. Charles Friss had joked about himself during the trial. And Sam, even Sam! *I stand corrected,* he'd said at the gallery. *I stand to the left, but I stand.*

"I believed in you from the very beginning," said the Asian man. "I told my wife that first night."

"I spoke to my children yesterday," said the woman who'd smiled to herself a lot. "I told them, 'I'll make sure these people do the right thing.'"

So, without looking the part, this woman and this man might have been the strongest people on the jury. Jack Frazier said that if the strongest and the second-strongest jurors are for you, you're home free.

"Did anybody want to vote for Dr. Niles?" I asked.

Pat hesitated. Was I prying too much? But then she said, "Will wasn't sure," and smiled at the man with spiky gray hair. "Maloo held out, too."

The chinless redhead, of course. "Maloo? What kind of name is that?"

"It's short for Marylou."

Charles Friss came back and headed straight for us. I figured he'd gone to the bank, to get the check for eleven million. But he didn't hand Loretta a check. "I wish you nothing but the best," Charles Friss told her, rather sincerely. To Jack Frazier he said, "As for you—next time."

Jack Frazier threw him a curt little nod.

Charles Friss coughed, spun around, and walked away briskly. I remembered a book of fairy tales I used to love as a kid. Every time a character had done all he was going to do, the author said, "He leaves our story here." I watched Charles Friss go through the swinging door.

There were hugs all around as the jurors said goodbye. Somebody had on perfume that smelled like grass and lavender. "Congratulations!" they called out as they left. "Good luck!" "Give Barry a kiss from us!"

I had to ask Hannes Leeser, "Who was the whiner? Maloo, right?"

Hannes Leeser shook his head. "The alternate," he said. "The young woman."

The blonde in braids. The drifter.

Jack Frazier gave me and Loretta a kind of group hug. I knew what that hug meant. But I couldn't bear for Jack Frazier to leave my story here.

"What do we do now?" I said. "Go to the bank and pick up our eleven million?"

"Elena!" Jack Frazier laughed. "That's not how it works. Those big verdicts you read about in the papers—nobody ever sees that kind of money. I'm afraid Judge Patterson will reduce the award." Something else they don't tell the jury. "Don't worry, it'll still add up to a lot: seven or eight million. Enough to build Barry his own group home. How's that for a good idea?"

"What about the appeal?" I said, not in the mood for good ideas. "Won't you still be our lawyer?"

"I do trial work," Jack Frazier said crisply. "For the appeal, you'll be assigned another lawyer."

Another lawyer! That was like Susie Brockleman's mother telling her to get another dog!

Then Jack Frazier, who was so good with words, fell silent. He looked at me the way he had long, long ago—only three weeks, but it felt like an ice age. He won't actually say good-bye, I realized. *We don't need words, you and I,* those spectacular green-brown eyes told me.

don't get me started

twenty-two

What did I do for the rest of the week? Drifted, like the blonde in braids, the whiner. I took long, lukewarm baths until I got as wrinkled as an empty tube of toothpaste. I did puzzles with Barry, but so distractedly he had to poke me. And I ran into Susie Brockleman and was shocked to see her yanking the leash of a big white standard poodle.

"Susie, you got another dog?" But you said you would never, never!

I heard Susie say something about "Misty Two."

"Two—like a sequel?"

"No!" Susie got a little annoyed. "Misty t-o-o. She's not a carbon copy, but another, entirely different Misty." Susie shook back her hair. "I'm growing it out," she said. "So, is your father home yet?"

"Next week," I said. So why did I tell Susie Brockleman,

of all people, about Barry's trial? Because that way I could say Jack Frazier's name.

Susie asked me, "Are you in love with your lawyer?"

This absolutely floored me. Roz might guess something like that—but Susie Brockleman? "Why do you ask?" I said, trying to sound confused.

"I saw *The Verdict*. That was about something medical too. Does your lawyer look like Paul Newman?"

I breathed out deeply. "No, he doesn't look anything like Paul Newman."

Just a lucky guess, Susie.

On Wednesday, a reporter from New York *Newsday* called and spoke to Loretta; on Thursday the paper printed a half-page article, under the headline, *Jury Awards Soho Boy 11 Mil in Malpractice Suit*.

Charles Friss was quoted. "We will appeal," he said (and probably coughed). "The jury was swept away by sympathy."

Loretta got a quote too. "I'm so appreciative that justice was done," she said.

By far the longest quote came from Jack Frazier. I could hear his voice so clearly in my head, his accent heavier than usual: "It was tragic, and the most tragic part was that Barry Gray's injuries were totally preventable. A little foresight, a little concern, a little care—it was all Barry Gray needed, and what he tragically didn't get."

That night, Aunt Beryl called up in a panic. "Did you see the article?" she asked me, breathlessly. "It mentions Barry's *name*. The neighborhood where he *lives*. The *money*, for God's sake." She paused. "Do you know what that means?"

I said I didn't.

"Barry could get kidnapped and held for ransom!" she whispered, as if maybe the phone were tapped. But couldn't a wiretapper hear a whisper, too? "It happened to my neighbor's friend. Her son won some money in Atlantic City—one of those freak things, where a fifty-cent machine pays off a hundred thousand dollars. Anyway, it got in all the papers, and a woman called him up and said, 'I'm moving to your block. Do you have children? Do they play outside your house, on your front lawn?' Doesn't that give you the creeps?"

Actually, it did, but I wasn't going to admit it. "She might have been telling the truth," I said.

"No one moved to the block, and the woman never called again," Aunt Beryl said, as if this was the chilling last line to a ghost story. "Ellen, listen. Keep Barry indoors for a month. You never know. Your Jack Frazier thought I ruined your case, remember? Maybe I'm not so wrong all the time."

I told Loretta about the call, and she thought it was ridiculous. Maribeth, who came to lunch the next day, didn't.

"I wouldn't keep Barry indoors," Maribeth said, spreading tuna salad on the onion bagels she'd bought downstairs. Miraculously a breeze came through our kitchen window on this muggy day. "But there are some strange people out there. Be careful if somebody calls up and asks about Barry. If he says he's a reporter, ask the name of the paper, look up the number, and call him back." Maribeth took a big bite. "What did you put in this, Ellen? It's out of this world."

"Honey mustard," I told her.

Loretta picked onion flakes off her bagel. She liked sesame. "As if we had eleven million stuffed in the sofa!" she said, frowning. "Ms. Hoffman at the law firm said if there's an appeal, we won't see any money for years. But whenever we see it, some of the money will be scattered in banks all over the city, in fifty-thousand-dollar clumps. And every time I want to withdraw any of it, I'll have to get written permission from Judge Patterson. Barry will get the rest of the money in lump sums when he's eighteen, twenty-five, and thirty. So any kidnappers are out of luck."

"Mom, you said *if* there's an appeal. But Charles Friss said it was definite."

"Ms. Hoffman told me the insurance company will probably offer to settle soon, for four or five million. If so, I'm taking it."

"But why?" I didn't mind the case dragging on and on, still somehow connected to Jack Frazier. "You never wanted to settle."

"Five million is a lot more than a hundred and fifty thousand," Loretta said. "Besides, there's a chance we'd lose everything on appeal. Jack Frazier's against it, but I'm looking out for you and Barry."

I couldn't believe it. Loretta was taking over. Jack Frazier was out of it.

Robert was shocked, of course. Stunned, was more like it. The trial wasn't supposed to have started—and it was all over? Eleven million! Are you serious?

We ordered in Chinese food on Robert's first night home, one week exactly after the trial ended. "I have thousands of questions," Robert said, slightly nasal with a cold. He always caught a cold, going from the practically sterile air of the submarine to the germ-happy air the rest of us breathe. "I want to hear every detail. Don't leave anything out."

So we told him everything, as best we could without a court reporter reading it all back to him. When I got to the part about my testimony, he said, "What a wonderful girl you are. What a wonderful woman you're going to be."

We told him about the duck that was really an eagle on top of the flagpole. I helped Barry eat some lo mein, which he then spit out—on my lap. "Too slippy," he muttered.

"*Slippery*," I said.

"I'm so proud of everyone," Robert said. "But I wish I'd been there!"

"Sweetheart, you were there every single moment," Loretta said, never afraid of the melodramatic.

"Egg roll," Barry said, reaching for one, missing it. On the second try he got it.

"Barry's a multimillionaire," I said. "Barry, do you care that you're a multimillionaire?"

"Money—for turtle food," Barry said.

I figured that was one way to spend it.

When Loretta told Robert about Dr. Niles's testimony, I could see Robert grow angry. "I can understand what it's like to be a doctor," he said. "The long years of training, the pressure. What I don't understand is a person who won't accept the consequences of his actions."

"The insurance companies don't allow the doctors to admit fault," Loretta said.

"But it was more than that," I said. And I told Robert my impression of Dr. Niles, how he could never believe he'd done anything wrong, that for him being imperfect was as likely as sea monsters attacking a submarine.

Robert nodded. "A person who can't ever learn anything about himself," he said.

I nodded back. Dr. Niles wasn't a whole person—he truly was a fraction. I didn't want to get stuck like that.

"It's something I've wondered about, how people learn about themselves," Robert said. "A friend on the boat told me that when you come home for a long shore leave, there's a short time when everything's so new again you find yourself learning all kinds of things. He called it 'a teachable moment.'"

Dr. Niles, Elena, Hannes Leeser, Dr. Underwood—all those people have given me glimpses of alternate futures, alternate ways of being. I nodded again.

twenty-three

That night Roz called from Maine. "Congratulations!" she boomed into the phone as I sat at the kitchen table.

"How did you find out?" I asked suspiciously.

"My dad sent me the clipping from *Newsday*. I had to call right away. Ellen, you won! Why do you sound miserable?"

"I won, and I lost," I said, staring at a stack of washed tinfoil platters from dinner, ready for the recycling bin downstairs. So where could I get my life recycled?

"What could you possibly lose after winning eleven million dollars?" Roz wanted to know.

I felt bad about not answering right away; this was a long-distance call. "I fell in love with our lawyer, Jack Frazier," I said at last.

Roz didn't miss a beat. "Isn't he a little old for you?"

"He's a very youthful person." Actually that didn't

describe him at all. How could I explain Jack Frazier? Only in terms of how he made me feel. "Roz, I once read an article about Japanese tidal waves. They're called tsunamis. Waves fifty feet high traveling at three hundred miles an hour. For me, Jack Frazier is like getting swept up in a wall of water moving as fast as a jet."

Roz said, "Is Jack Frazier that good-looking?"

"Not at all," I said. "His hair is—well, it's bristly, and his eyebrows are bushy, and his face is all bony." I paused. "His eyes are incredible, though."

Roz laughed. "Not exactly heartthrob material. Is he really nice, then?"

"Only when he wants to be. He's got a terrible temper. Not much of a sense of humor, either." The way Roz was breathing, I could sense disapproval. "He's a passionate person, you see."

"So far I don't see," Roz said.

"I guess I should also mention that he's married and has two daughters."

Now it was Roz's turn for a long-distance pause. "Ellie," she said finally, "what was it about Jack Frazier that pulled you under like a Japanese tidal wave?"

I said, "He's very . . . capable."

"How romantic! Is he punctual, too?"

"Roz, capable was what I wanted! When you're starving, you don't want a meal at a four-star restaurant." You just want an onion bagel with fresh mozzarella and anchovies, I was thinking, during yet another expensive silence. I looked at our yellow walls, slightly sun-streaked.

"You're a capable person," Roz told me easily.

"Don't I wish! I could never take care of myself and also Barry—"

"Ellie, you don't have to take care of Barry right this minute. Years from now you'll have to help supervise Barry's life. Years from now! And now you have eleven million dollars to help you do it!"

It wouldn't actually be that much, but I didn't want to get technical on her. "Jack Frazier thought I could create a group home for Barry," I said. "A place where he'd live with a few other people, and a small staff. What do you think?"

I remembered how Roz had imagined Barry out in the country somewhere, writing poetry. She said, "I think it's the best idea since talking pictures."

I didn't have to tell Roz how much she meant to me. She knew it.

"Nellie! Nellie!" Barry called from the living room.

"Speaking of talking pictures, I promised Barry we'd watch the movie tonight." Of course, I didn't have to say which one.

"Something just occurred to me," Roz said. "Supposedly the Wizard is exposed as an old fraud, somebody who only pretends to be great and powerful. But he really is great and powerful! In his subtle, ingenious way, he empowers all the others." I could feel her smile. "Ellie, maybe Jack Frazier was your first real love. But he won't be your last."

"You think I should go out with the Wizard of Oz?"

"No, the Tin Man," she said, laughing. "You both have such big, breakable hearts. Actually I was thinking of somebody with one quality your passionate, capable lawyer doesn't have—the ability to love you back."

Funny she should mention the Tin Man. He'd always been my favorite character. He started out feeling empty and hollow, and he ended up whole.

In bed that night I thought about the group home. It could be like a country house in the middle of the city, a place where people could write poetry if they wanted to. Such places are expensive, Dr. Hunter had said. Well, we had millions. Such places have long waiting lists, she said, too. Not at the Barry Gray House. There was no wait at all.

Without my noticing, I fell asleep without the duck lamp on.

Wednesday afternoon, calm, cloudless. Barry was in his room with Claire; Robert had to report to a naval office downtown. As for me, I hadn't seen Jack Frazier in eight whole days.

When Loretta came home from work, I was on the couch, flipping through a cookbook where every recipe required yogurt. "Why don't we invite Jack Frazier over for dinner tomorrow night?" I said. "I can make turkey tetrazzini."

Loretta frowned at me. "You mean, Jack Frazier and his wife and children, too?"

I didn't say anything.

"Besides, tomorrow's an opening at the gallery."

I put down the cookbook. "I'm on hiatus—like they say about a TV show when they don't know whether to cancel it."

"El, you love working there!"

"I'm not ready," I said with a world-weary sigh. "That trial was so overwhelming . . . maybe I'm getting a fever . . . "

"He wouldn't come, El." Loretta was firm. "Jack Frazier's business with us is over." She emphasized *business*. "He's probably deeply involved in another case by now."

Deeply involved. That was Jack Frazier, all right. "Is a teenage girl part of that one too?"

Loretta looked to the ceiling. "How should I know?"

"Mom, don't you miss Jack Frazier at all?"

Loretta sat beside me, placing her long, graceful, cool fingers on my arm. How could her hand be so cool, in August? "You'll be a senior this year," she said. "Does that feel scary?"

"No," I said.

"Even so, maybe you don't need to take on so much anymore. Senior year can be fun." Need to take on, she'd said. "Are you unhappy about Ray?"

"A little." She knew about the imminent breakup. But we both knew this wasn't because of Ray.

"Why, honey, why?" Loretta said. "Why Jack Frazier?"

So I told her, just the way I'd told Roz. How passionate Jack Frazier was, how capable.

Loretta nodded. "Like Sam," she said.

"What!" I pulled my arm away as if her hand had become a hot iron. "I thought you wanted to talk, Mom, really talk! That you wanted to really understand about me and Jack Frazier!"

"I do, honey. You've been so blinded by Jack Frazier, you haven't noticed that a passionate, capable person has in the meantime fallen head over heels for you."

I stood up, energy like lightning flooding my body. Why was Loretta saying such things? "Sam is nothing like Jack Frazier," I said, as slowly and calmly as I could. "Sam is sullen and moody—and empty and hollow," I threw in.

"Used to be," Loretta said. "Sam changed—quite a while ago, El, but you never noticed."

I had to sit down again. I had to make her understand.

"I promise you," Loretta said, "in time, all you'll feel for Jack Frazier is grateful that he won Barry's case. All the rest will melt away."

"Mom, I used to worry that Barry would turn out like Sam!"

"El, Sam came to the trial every day. Why? When you testified, he positively glowed. Why? When the verdict was read, he broke down. Why? If I have to hit you over the head with it, I will."

I groaned. "I feel like I've been hit over the head—it hurts. Sam's so difficult! He's like a tiger—it would be like training a tiger—"

"Sounds like something you'd be good at."

"Mom, he has cerebral palsy!"

"Maribeth said that in relationships between the handicapped and the not-handicapped, the chances of success are the same as in so-called normal-normal relationships."

Right—terrible! "That's not what I meant," I said. "Barry has cerebral palsy. Sam has cerebral palsy. I don't know if I want all that cerebral palsy in my life."

"Neither does Barry. Neither does Sam. Besides, Sam won't need a guardian the way Barry will. El, what if Dr. Hunter is wrong? What if Barry can fall in love someday? Wouldn't you want somebody as wonderful as you to fall in love with Barry?"

Robert had said I was wonderful, too. A wonderful girl on her way to becoming a wonderful woman. "I don't feel particularly wonderful," I groaned. What was it Dr. Niles had said at the trial about my birth? *Complications none.* Why couldn't that apply to the whole rest of my life

and not just the first few minutes? *Complications plenty.*
That was far more accurate. And there was nothing I could
do about it except get ready for more complications when
they showed up, as unexpectedly as Aunt Beryl in the
courtroom.

"We could invite Sam over for turkey tetrazzini tomorrow night," Loretta suggested.

I picked up the cookbook. "Bring to a boil," I read
aloud. "Stir constantly with a wire whisk." I looked up at
Loretta, at her gray-blue eyes, at my mother, who had
made a trial happen just for me. "This recipe is very . . .
complicated," I said. "If Sam wants turkey tetrazzini, he'll
have to help out. And if he gives me a hard time, the whole
thing's off!"

Sam didn't give me a hard time.

Lois Metzger grew up in Queens, New York, and now lives in Greenwich Village with her husband, the writer Tony Hiss, and their son, Jacob. She has written articles and short stories for *The New Yorker*, *Omni*, *The Nation*, *Harper's Bazaar*, and *The North American Review*. *Ellen's Case* is the sequel to her first novel, *Barry's Sister*, also published by Puffin.